approximately Yours

approximately Yours

JULIE HAMMERLE

Entangled Publishing, LLC
2614 South Timberline Road
Suite 109
Fort Collins, CO 80525
Visit our website at www.entangledpublishing.com.

Crush is an imprint of Entangled Publishing, LLC.

Edited by Kate Brauning
Cover design by Cover Couture
Cover art from Bigstock

Manufactured in the United States of America

First Edition October 2017

CRUSH

To Trixie, my Christmas baby

To my cousins:
Patti, Keith, Dan, Meg, Erik, Pat, Jill, Kari, Tim, Ryan,
Sam, Taren, Ben, Tori, and Tyler

Chapter One

Thursday, December 7

The reporter from the *Minneapolis Star-Tribune* had been following Danny Garland around since the moment he pulled into the North Pole High School parking lot for basketball practice. The guy trailed Danny into the school, then into the locker room and out to the bench. Now he hovered next to Danny on the sidelines while he double knotted his shoes. "What's it like living in North Pole?" the reporter asked, his stale tobacco breath filling Danny's nose. "Do you eat fruitcake all day? Do you know the perfect recipe for eggnog?"

Danny knotted his laces, ignoring the phone the reporter used as a recording device. "No North Pole questions," he'd said back in the parking lot. Danny's hometown was all this dude wanted to talk about.

"What did you ask Santa for this year? Have you been a good boy?"

Danny tapped the top of his shoe and stood from his

crouch. He had a game to prepare for. All this interest in North Pole was a distraction he didn't need. The reporter, a dumpy middle-aged man with a scraggly neck beard, scrambled to keep up with Danny's long legs as he made his way onto the court for warm-ups. Danny rolled his eyes at his brother Brian, who was hanging out on the sidelines. This reporter nonsense was his fault. Brian fancied himself Danny's "manager" and was the one who'd set up this interview without Danny's okay.

"No disrespect." The reporter slid a few feet on the freshly waxed gym floor. Several of Danny's teammates, who were already out on the court, chuckled. They were laughing at Danny as much as at the reporter. They thought Danny had picked this day on purpose for his interview—an afternoon when the poms were practicing as well as the basketball team. It totally looked like Danny was begging for attention.

"I'm just curious. North Pole High has never been in contention for the state tournament before, and, frankly, until Stan Stashiuk joined the NHL, the sports world had no idea this place existed."

"Well, it does." Brian stepped onto the court and tossed his little brother a fresh water bottle. "Stash put us on the map, and Danny is going to keep us there."

After taking a sip, Danny handed the water back to his brother. Then he grabbed a ball from the rack, dribbled twice, and banked a shot from just beyond the three-point arc. He'd leave Brian to handle this reporter from the cities, who cared more about playing up the small town angle than focusing on Danny's, and his team's, actual talent. They were fresh off a big win against the reigning state champions that had shocked the entire Minnesota sports world. Now the North Pole Reindeer was a team to be reckoned with, due in no small part to Danny's contribution at power forward.

"I do want to play up the North Pole angle, just a bit."

The reporter followed Brian, the chattier Garland, back to the bench, and Danny pretended not to notice. He glanced toward the corner of the gym and caught sight of his long-time girlfriend, Star, leading the red and green-clad poms squad in warm ups. He gave her a quick wave, which she didn't return. Danny normally wouldn't have noticed the slight. The two of them had been dating since junior high—*six years*. Their relationship had evolved past worrying about perceived snubs. They were solid. At least they used to be.

Lately he couldn't tell.

However, now was not the time for girlfriend-related paranoia. Staying focused on tonight's game was the important thing. Maintaining his image as the captain of the basketball team, boyfriend to the head cheerleader, and North Pole's current golden boy was the only way he'd ever escape this town. He was not some Podunk hick who bought into all of North Pole's Christmas garbage. The *Minneapolis Star Tribune* would not make that his narrative, not when he was heading into the most important season of his life, and not when, thanks to the team's early success, colleges were actually traveling to North Pole to check him out. All of this stuff bonded him and Star. They were the golden couple. They were going to get out. He was not going to be stuck here for his entire life like his big brother.

"Danny used to win the gingerbread contest every single year." Brian spoke right into the reporter's phone.

The hell? Glaring at his mouthy brother, Danny hurled the ball at him.

Smiling sheepishly, Brian tossed the ball back. "Sorry, Dan. I forgot. We're not supposed to talk about that."

No, they weren't supposed to talk about that. That was another lifetime. That was a part of Danny that no longer existed. He was not going to be seen as the cutesy little basketball player from a Christmas village who held the record for most consecutive gingerbread competition wins. He was here to play basketball and kick ass. Full stop.

The reporter shuffled over to Danny, careful not to slide around in his loafers. "Okay, so you don't want to talk about your gingerbread skills. Can we discuss your basketball bonafides instead?"

"Gladly." Danny sank another three-pointer from near the baseline while the rest of the team warmed up around him.

"You shoot like Steph Curry, you rebound like Rodman in his prime, and you look like freaking Christian Laettner." The reporter caught his breath. "Is there anything you can't do?"

I can't get my girlfriend to wave to me. "Of course," Danny said.

"Care to elaborate?" The reporter held his phone toward Danny's lips.

"He can't dunk," Brian shouted from the sidelines.

Danny stopped dribbling, tucked the ball under his arm, and glared at his brother. "I can dunk."

Brian shook his head. "Since when?"

"Since forever." Danny rolled his eyes again. Brian was more of a liability than an asset at this point. They were going to have to talk about some things before the next game.

"Please. I've never seen you." Brian was totally playing him right now. He'd seen Danny dunk millions of times. Heck, Danny had dunked over Brian when they were shooting hoops in the driveway just last week.

Danny's shoulders dropped. "Dude. Yes, you have."

Brian stared into the middle distance as if his mind were running through every time he'd ever watched Danny on a basketball court. Danny could have strangled him. Brian was trying to get him to showboat in front of this reporter, his teammates, and Star. "I've literally never seen you dunk."

"You know how you could clear this up." The reporter cocked his head toward the basket.

Sighing, Danny made his way to the free throw line. He wasn't a show-off, but he wasn't one to back down from a challenge, either. At least this dunking drama had distracted the reporter from the North Pole questions. Danny dribbled the ball a few times, psyching himself up while glancing over at two of his teammates, Kevin and Marcus, who were playing a little one-on-one just off to his right.

He tuned out the noises in the gym—the shouts, the cheers, the band warming up in the corner—and focused with tunnel vision on the basket. Giving up on any pretense of playing by the rules, Danny cradled the ball, ran toward the basket, and leaped into the air. Upon takeoff, his foot slipped on the freshly waxed floor, but he kept going—up, up, up. He grasped the rim with one hand, chucked the ball through the net with the other, and lost his grip. His hands fought for purchase, but for nothing. Danny was falling, and Kevin, who'd managed to get around Marcus, barreled right at him. Danny bent his knees to land gracefully, but the slippery floor sent his legs flying, and Kevin landed squarely on his right shin.

The last thing Danny remembered was the sickening crack as his tibia broke in two.

• • •

Friday, December 15

"I mean, how can you not love this place?" Holly and her cousin Elda had just walked past a gun store called "And to All a Good Night." A nativity scene decorated the front window with the wise men holding assault rifles instead of gold, frankincense, and myrrh. This town was kitschy perfection.

"I know, right?" Elda bit into the warm chocolate croissant she'd initially called a "calorie bomb" when they'd picked up a few at Sugarplum Sweets a few minutes ago. Holly hadn't hesitated for a second. Chocolate croissants were tradition, and tradition equaled negative calories. The next two weeks of her life would be full of tradition.

When she was a kid, Holly used to believe this small town in Minnesota was the actual North Pole. All the shops were Christmas themed. The clothing boutique was called Mrs. Claus's Closet. The gas station went by Reindeer Fueling Station. People from all across the country made the pilgrimage here year after year like it was a religious experience, like Christmas didn't exist unless it came with snowman cookies from the bakery, eggnog from the local pub, and a photo with Santa in the town square.

This place had felt like magic back then, and, if Holly was being honest, it still did. Maybe it was because she hadn't been back here since she was ten. All her memories were good ones, preserved in her mind under a red and green glow.

Speaking of... She scanned the people they passed on the sidewalk, hunting for one person in particular, one boy she hoped to run into. Danny Garland. He'd be wearing a cast right now. Yeah, she'd done the stalkery thing and googled him. And, yeah, she felt completely pathetic about it.

"It kind of feels like Grandma's still here, doesn't it?" Elda asked. "This place smells like her." Elda breathed in deeply.

"Or she smelled like it." Cinnamon and cloves. The scent transported Holly to the couch in her grandmother's den, where the two of them used to cuddle together and plot out their gingerbread contest plans. The scent of North Pole was pure, unadulterated nostalgia.

Holly hadn't been back in eight years, but being here now, it was like she'd never left. Her family had stopped coming to North Pole for Christmas once the kids got older and everyone got too busy. With sports and school functions and the cost of it all, it became harder and harder for Holly's family to make the trip from Illinois to Minnesota, and for her aunt's and uncle's crews to make their trips from Vermont and California. Holly's dad and his siblings started paying to fly Grandma around the country for the holidays. She'd spend Thanksgiving in Los Angeles, Christmas in Chicago, and New Year's in Vermont. It had made life easier for the adults, but it had kept Holly and her cousins away from each other.

She and Elda had seen each other for the first time since they were in middle school a month ago at their Grandma's funeral in California, where she'd passed away. Back when they were kids, Holly had known Elda as "Esme," but she'd changed her nickname because "everyone goes by Esme now. It's so bougie. Thanks, *Twilight*."

To which Holly had responded, "*Twilight* ruins everything." Holly was mostly neutral on the existence of *Twilight*, but she jumped at the chance to bond with her cousin. The two girls hit it off marvelously, spending the next few weeks chatting and texting, reminiscing about their childhood memories, and making big plans for what to do in North Pole over the holidays when their families would make one last pilgrimage here to clean out Grandma's home and prepare to sell it.

Elda had actually brought up Danny Garland in a text conversation a few weeks ago. She'd sent Holly a picture from one of their trips to North Pole with the message, "Remember this dorky kid?"

Holly played it off like she hadn't. "Yeah, total dork," she'd said.

Thinking about Danny Garland had been the only thing keeping her from utter despair over losing her grandma.

She'd spent the past few weeks leading up to her family's trip to North Pole imagining all the ways she might run into Danny—she'd know him right away, of course, but he'd know her, too, the girl who used to enter the gingerbread contest with her grandmother, the girl who came in second place to him three years running, the girl he'd smiled at sheepishly from across the room after their last competition. That smile was etched on her brain.

"I'm sad there's no snow, though." Elda held up a hand as if to catch a non-existent snowflake.

It was the middle of December in Minnesota, and Holly wasn't even wearing a coat. She'd pulled a chunky sweater over the powder blue A-line dress she'd paired with green low-top Chuck Taylors, but that was it. Chicago had been the same before she left—too warm. Holly wanted snow. She wanted Christmas. This wasn't Christmas. "Global warming is almost as bad as *Twilight*," she said, calling back to their earlier conversation.

"Oh my God, oh my God, oh my God!" Elda stopped in her tracks.

"What?" Holly craned her neck over her cousin's shoulder to see what Elda was so excited about. Elda crouched down, and the grizzly scene revealed itself—a dead, mangled squirrel. Holly backed up on instinct. "Ew."

"Not 'ew.'" Elda examined it. "The intestines look like blooming roses."

Well, that was one way to look at it. Holly grabbed Elda's arm and dragged her up. "Whatever you say, my friend. Let's grab some coffee." Holly crossed the threshold into Santabucks, where she immediately halted in her tracks.

"You okay?" Elda skirted around Holly, leaving her standing in the doorway alone.

Holly managed to choke out a "fine" as she stared at the ghost from her past. She'd let her guard down for a minute to think about global warming and a dead squirrel, and now here he was.

Danny Garland was wiping down the counter. *The* Danny Garland. Holly had seen his recent photos online, so she was prepared for the hotness. Modern day Danny was perfection. The dorkiness was a faint memory. He no longer wore glasses. His sandy brown hair was perfectly tousled, and his arrow-like, angular nose pointed straight down to plump, pouty lips.

Danny hadn't noticed Holly at all, at least not really. He'd glanced at her for a second, then fixed his eyes on Elda.

Holly's world crumbled around her. The ideal scenario she'd imagined, where Danny caught sight of her, remembered their connection as kids, and fell madly and deeply in love with her, was utter fiction. Holly was the dumbass who'd failed to see the obvious. She and Elda had looked like twins when they were younger (tall, skinny girls with brown hair and brown eyes), but puberty had been much kinder to Elda. Holly's cousin had blemish-free olive skin and medium brown hair that was so shiny it defied scientific explanation. She was the girl next door of every boy's dreams. Holly was the girl next door who actually lived next door. Of course he was checking out Elda. Anyone with eyes would have done the same.

Holly hunched her shoulders. She'd been a fool to expect him to recognize her. She was no one. And she was not the girl she'd been at ten. Back then, she'd been a bean pole with long, brown pigtails. Now she was curvy—okay, "plus-size"— with red statement glasses and dyed jet-black hair, which she'd had chopped into a bowl cut after getting ill-advised bangs that parted in the middle and swooped out to the side like little wings no matter what she did. Her tongue touched the tiny scar that bisected her upper lip. It was a nervous reaction, something she did all the time without thinking.

"What can I get you?" Danny stared right into Elda's eyes, clearly under her spell. "And you." He nodded slightly toward Holly, but he didn't take his eyes off Elda. That was about right. Holly's daydreams had led predictably to disappointment. Again.

"Half skim, half two percent, half caf, no foam latte with one Splenda and one Sugar in the Raw. Extra hot." Elda blushed a bit on the word "hot."

"Got it." Danny typed the order into the computer. Then he turned to Holly and waited expectantly for her order.

Holly searched for a hint of recognition, but nope. It was official. Danny Garland, the guy she'd been dreaming about—off and on, she wasn't *that* pathetic—for the past eight years, had no idea who she was. "Iced cinnamon latte," Holly said. "Two percent. With whipped." She'd drown her disappointment in sugar and milk fat. Maybe that, too, counted as negative calories. Eating one's feelings was a tradition of sorts.

Elda leaned against the counter in a way that Holly assumed was supposed to be casual. "So, North Pole, am I right?" She said it like a bad actress in a bad movie trying to read her lines, moving her body deliberately, as if she'd forgotten how to control the muscles in her arms and face.

Danny didn't watch her display, which was probably a lucky thing for Elda. He seemed too busy focusing on his task at hand—navigating the tiny space behind the espresso machine while on crutches. "North Pole," he said in agreement.

To which Elda replied, "North. Pole."

This was perhaps the most pathetic mating ritual Holly had ever witnessed. Every cell inside her body groaned in second-hand embarrassment for her cousin. Maybe Holly didn't have the physique of a model, but at least she knew how to talk to a guy and not give off the impression that she was an alien trying its darnedest to impersonate human interactions.

Danny glanced up at Elda with a faint smile. Holly couldn't tell if he was patronizing her or if he was truly interested in seeing this banal conversation through to its conclusion.

Elda batted her eyelashes. Ah, she was bringing out the big guns, going in for the kill. Holly started picturing herself as a bridesmaid at their wedding. She'd survive it. She'd give a lovely toast, relaying Danny and Elda's meet-cute to a few hundred guests. But then Elda said, "I found a really mangled dead squirrel in the street outside."

Danny, no doubt alarmed by Elda's unorthodox idea of foreplay, dropped one of his crutches.

Holly, without even thinking, dashed behind the counter and rescued the crutch from the floor.

"I have a girlfriend." Danny looked right at Holly, as if enlisting her help, like he was expecting her to break the news gently to her roadkill-obsessed cousin. "I really do. I have a girlfriend."

"Okay." *Whatever, Danny, we got it. You're not single.* "Here." Holly handed him his crutch.

"Thanks." Danny's eyes softened. He was staring right at Holly, and now her insides were melting for a whole new reason. His eyes were a striking blue, but it was more than that. She could sense Original Danny behind those eyes. His brilliant brain hid behind those eyes, analyzing the situation, working through this cousin-related foolishness. "I like your glasses," he said finally.

Holly opened her mouth to introduce herself, to tell him she knew him back when, but she held back. She'd been thinking about Danny forever—she'd googled him, for goodness' sake—but he didn't remember her. He hadn't been waiting around, pining over her for years. He had a girlfriend.

He *really* had a girlfriend. Holly handed him the crutch and retreated to her rightful place on the other side of the counter.

When he finished their order, the girls grabbed their drinks and left the shop. Elda smacked herself on the forehead after the door to Santabucks had shut behind them. "Gah, he's so cute! Maybe I should've gotten his name instead of talking about squirrel carcasses."

"Danny," Holly blurted, her eyes down on her beverage.

"Danny? How do you know that?"

Holly clamped her mouth shut for a moment. She'd tipped her hand. "Um...Elda, that was Danny Garland, the dorky kid from the gingerbread competition." She made sure to emphasize the word "dorky."

"That was Danny?" Elda spun around and stared at the door to Santabucks.

"That was Danny."

"Well, he got cute."

"Nah," Holly said. "I didn't notice." She'd never admit to her cousin the eight-year torch she'd carried for Danny Garland, beautiful human and king of the gingerbread contest. She'd never tell anyone that, because it was sad and moot. She'd imagined a connection eight years ago. Holly had been living that lie for too long.

"Well, I did notice," Elda said, "and I made a complete fool of myself. As I do."

Holly dropped a few coins into the bucket next to an elf collecting donations for the local food pantry. "You were fine." *Ah, the lies we tell our loved ones.*

"I was a complete goober, like always," Elda said. "And you were cool as a cucumber."

Holly glanced up at her cousin, who was blowing across the lid of her beverage, making a low whistling sound. "Hey, Elda."

Elda stopped blowing on her drink and looked up.

Holly wiped her cheek. "You've got something on your face there."

"Shoot." Elda spun around and peered into the window of the nearest storefront, the flower shop. Using the window as a mirror, she wiped away the smudge on her cheek. "God, I'm so awkward. Do you think Danny noticed?"

"No way." Holly linked arms with her cousin. "He was definitely looking at you, but I'm positive the chocolate on your cheek was the last thing on his mind."

Elda rested her head on Holly's shoulder. "I wish I had half your chill around guys."

Chill was all Holly had. It was self-preservation. "And I'd love to be half as hot as you are." Holly had always assumed girls like Elda had it so easy—that all they had to do was exist, and they'd get any guy they wanted. But it wasn't as simple as that. Elda still had her insecurities. She didn't care about sports or music or movies. She found beauty in the things other people found disgusting. She enjoyed exploring the guts of almost everything—animals, cars, houses. The grosser and more covered in hair and scum, the happier she was. But those weren't easy topics to pursue in the early stages of a relationship.

"Holly, you're totally hot. Shut up. You're a badass and an individual. Looks like mine can only get you so far. If we Frankenstein-ed your keen sense of what not to say with my hair and boobs, we'd be unstoppable," Elda said. "The perfect woman."

They totally would be. A girl with Holly's savvy and Elda's body would be more powerful than Wonder Woman. "We'd rule the freaking world. A guy like Danny Garland wouldn't know what hit him."

Chapter Two

Star was thirty minutes late.

Danny checked his phone again. No texts from her or anyone. Yet another way Danny was failing with women today. He couldn't stop thinking about how he'd blurted out "I have a girlfriend!" like a jerk when he thought that girl was flirting with him in Santabucks. Oh, and then he complimented the other girl's glasses in a way that had her looking at him like he'd just told her he wanted to make a skin suit out of her. Danny's game with the ladies was seriously lacking at the moment, not that it was ever something to write home about.

He grabbed a fleece and went out onto the porch to wait for Star. He checked his phone again. They were going to miss their movie.

A minivan rolled down the street and slowed to a stop in front of Danny's house. As the passenger's side window slowly descended, the face of the Reindeer's center, Marcus Carter, came into view.

"Hey, Cap," Marcus yelled. "What are you doing out here?"

"Waiting for Star," Danny said. "Have you seen her?"

"Sure. The poms were practicing the same time we were. We're all meeting at the arcade. Girls, too." Marcus nodded toward the empty passenger's seat. "Come on."

"Star didn't mention plans with me?" Danny said.

"Nope."

Maybe Danny'd had the date wrong, or they'd gotten their signals crossed. He had been kind of off ever since his accident. Since school got out last week, he'd had no routine. He was definitely reading too much into Star not being here. It was a scheduling mishap, full stop. Danny was just feeling insecure after his very embarrassing encounter with two cute girls in the coffee shop today.

"I'll come, too. It'll be fun." Danny nestled his crutches under one arm, grabbed the railing, and hopped down the stairs on one leg. Marcus jumped out of the car right away and tried to help, but Danny had already reached the sidewalk.

"You've mastered those crutches, Cap." Marcus walked with Danny to the minivan and loaded his crutches into the back seat. "No surprise there."

As Marcus got behind the wheel, Danny bit back questions about the team, even though he was dying to know how practice had gone, if the Reindeer were ready for the first round of the winter break tournament in Countryside two days from now. Any answer would gut him. He couldn't guess which would hurt more—to hear they were doing fine without him or that they were in dire straits because of his ill-advised dunk attempt.

"You coming to the game Sunday?" Marcus turned onto Main Street. It was only about four blocks from Danny's house to the arcade. The street lamps were on but were almost unnecessary with the powerful electric glow emanating from all the houses decked out for Christmas.

"I don't know." Danny scratched an itch just under the edge of his cast, something he did about six hundred times a day lately. He walked around with a pen over his ear for just this purpose. Epic under-cast scratching had taken basketball's place in his life.

"You should come, Cap. You're good luck. We need all the luck we can get."

Did he mean they needed luck because they sucked without him, or because luck was a good thing, generally? "I'll think about it," Danny said. "And I'm not 'Cap' anymore." All the younger members of the team called him that. "Kevin is 'Cap' now."

"Once the captain, always the captain," Marcus said. "Hoping I'll be 'Cap' next year."

"I bet you will be." Danny'd had that same anticipation during his junior year, and now he'd been relegated to the sidelines.

Kevin Snow met them just inside the arcade, Santa's Playhouse. "You made it. They're already in the laser tag room." He glanced at Danny's leg and winced. "Sorry, Dan."

In his quest to find Star, Danny hadn't even thought about what they might be doing at the arcade. Of course they were playing laser tag, something Danny couldn't do. They couldn't just be sitting at one of the tabletop *Donkey Kong* games eating pizza. "No worries," Danny said. "We'll meet up when you're done."

"We're only playing a round or two." Marcus waved as he followed Kevin toward the laser tag room in the back of the arcade.

Utterly alone and feeling conspicuous, Danny went to a kiosk and purchased a game card for himself. Then he dragged a stool over to the *Pac-Man* machine, sat down, and started the first level. He died on the second frame, after playing for less than five minutes. He'd never been a big video game guy because he'd been too busy playing sports to invest any time in them. And Danny generally didn't bother doing things if he might fail.

Familiar faces popped out at Danny amid the packs of tourists. Sam Anderson and his girlfriend, Tinka, were over by the Skee-Ball games. Elena Chestnut and Oliver Prince were eating cheeseless pizza while playing *Q*bert*. All couples. Danny had to find Star. He was missing an appendage right now.

He grabbed his crutches and bee-lined it for the laser tag room. "I want in," he told Dinesh, one of the twenty-something guys who'd stuck around in North Pole after high school. He was working tonight as the laser-tag gatekeeper.

"You're on crutches." Dinesh folded his arms over his green, red, and white striped uniform. Everyone who worked at Santa's Playhouse had to dress like an actual elf.

A voice from behind Danny said, "You can't go in there if you're on crutches."

Danny's head swung around. Dinesh's best friend, Craig, sat alone at a table, eating pizza and drinking Mellow Yellow.

"You don't make the rules, Craig," Danny said.

"He doesn't," Dinesh agreed, "but he is correct. No crutches." He pointed to the gold star on his uniform. "I'm shift manager."

"He takes his job very seriously," Craig said.

Danny dropped his crutches and hopped on his good foot over to the door. The calf muscle on his left leg was going to be double the size of his right by the time he finally got his cast off. "No crutches. Let me in."

"I don't think so," Dinesh said.

"You're a liability," Craig added.

"I'm not going to do anything. I'm not even gonna play. I'm just going to sit behind a barrier and watch. All my friends are in there. Please, Dinesh." Pleading to Craig would've been in vain. "I'll give you free coffee for a month."

Craig and Dinesh shared a look. Craig shook his head no, but Dinesh pulled open the door. "I'm putting my job on the line for you."

"I know," Danny said. "And thank you."

"Stay on the floor," Dinesh said. "You're a spectator only."

Danny saluted him and hopped into a dark hallway as the door shut behind him. He pulled open the next door, and strobing neon lights assaulted him. He bounced in and grabbed the arm of the first person he saw—Marcus—both to get his attention and to hold himself up.

"What are you doing here, Cap?" Marcus asked. "You're gonna get hurt."

"I just want to hang out. Help me sit down somewhere, please."

He put his arm around Marcus's shoulders, and the two of them made their way over to a little fort in the middle of the room. "Stay safe," Marcus said, as he helped Danny sit on a foam bench in front of the main fortress, then hustled away in pursuit of their point guard.

Hunting for Star, Danny glanced around. A trio of cheerleaders chased the point guard up a ramp. Kevin shot the school mascot right in the chest. But no Star. A sick feeling formed in his gut.

Danny should've stayed out in the arcade. Really, he should've stayed home. This was stupid. Star was probably parked in front of his house right now.

From inside the fort behind him, Danny heard a crash followed by a giggle. He whirled around and caught sight of his girlfriend's platinum blond braid glowing blue in the black light. She had her arms around someone else, and Danny's stomach lurched when he realized who it was.

"Phil?"

The team's student trainer, Phil Waterston, and Star pushed each other away at the same time.

"Danny!" Star wiped her lips with the back of her hand. "What are you doing here?"

Good thing Danny was sitting, because this had knocked his entire world off balance. He couldn't decide whether to cry or punch the foam barrier in front of him. "I could ask you the same thing. We're supposed to be on a date."

Her hand flew to her mouth. "Oh my God, I forgot."

"Apparently." Danny tried to push himself up, but he found nothing nearby to grab for balance. His good leg shook from the shock. Star and Phil. Phil and Star. Phil Waterston, the guy who had sat by Danny's side on the floor while they waited for an ambulance not even two weeks ago.

Phil dashed out of the fort and grabbed Danny's elbow before he could topple over, but Danny pushed him away while simultaneously grasping for the nearest cheerleader—a freshman. She helped him stand.

"Danny, I'm sorry," Phil said. "It just…happened."

It just…happened. It just…*happened* that his girlfriend—the person he'd been closest to for the past *six years*—was cheating on him. The cheerleader helped Danny over to a foam barrier, where he rested his hands to keep balance as the girl ran off to find her friends.

"It just happened in the middle of a crowded room where all our friends were hanging out?" That was almost the worst part. They didn't even have the decency to mess around in private. Anyone could've seen. They didn't even care if Danny found out, or if they hurt him. "This wasn't the first time, was it?"

"Yes, it was," Star said. She remained in the doorway of the fort. She hadn't run over to help Danny or plead with him. She'd kept her distance and let Phil handle the fallout.

This was the person Danny had chosen to be with for six years—someone who'd cheat on him without hesitation and then let her new guy act as cleanup crew.

Phil glared at Star. "No, it wasn't. But we only ever kissed, that's it."

Danny's brain stalled on the image of Star and Phil—*Phil!*—intertwined. He waved his arms, but he almost toppled over. "I really don't need the details. I…" He turned to Star as he clutched the barrier to stay upright. "Why didn't you tell me? Why didn't you just break up with me?"

She frowned and glanced at his leg. "Danny."

"Oh, good. You stayed with me out of pity. Super." She didn't care about him. Maybe she'd never cared about him. "Well, I guess this saves you from having to be the bad guy." Danny glanced around, searching for Marcus or Kevin or anyone who might be able to help him to the door. Everyone stayed hidden, either as part of the game or to avoid blowback from the Danny/Star/Phil triangle. Danny hopped toward the exit. He had to do this on his own.

"Seriously, Danny. Let me help you." Phil reached for Danny's arm.

Danny yanked it away. "I'm fine, *Phil*." He had to get out of here. His entire chest tightened, like it was about to burst into ugly, blubbering tears. He couldn't cry in front of his entire team, and he definitely couldn't break down in front of Star.

Using columns of neon padding as his lifeline, Danny bounced on one leg across the floor and out the door.

"Have fun?" asked Dinesh.

"Best time ever." Still wobbling on his shaky leg, Danny retrieved his crutches from Dinesh and scanned the floor. Sam and Oliver were still here, but they were with their girlfriends. Everyone was with their girlfriends, something Danny no longer had, which was a completely foreign concept to him. He could barely remember not having a girlfriend. He'd taken Star being his girlfriend for granted, like he'd taken having two unbroken legs for granted. Eyes stinging, he limped to the door and out onto Main Street, which, at least, was snow free. He felt like a spectacle, a sad, girlfriend-less sack with a broken leg.

And, ha-ha, it wasn't like getting a new girlfriend would be an easy task for him. He couldn't even have a normal conversation with two strangers in a coffee shop. This was the first day of his new life as a loner.

Tourists pranced down the sidewalk, peering into shop windows, carrying armloads of green, red, and gold shopping bags. Danny lowered his eyes and booked it to the end of the street.

Single. He was single now, something he hadn't been in, like, forever. For as long as he or the collective consciousness of North Pole could remember, they'd always been "Danny and Star" or "Star and Danny." Wherever one went, the other followed. Her friends were his friends and his friends were her friends. Their lives were intertwined to the point where untangling them would be impossible.

Danny bit his lip. He would not cry. Not here. But then the tears started rolling down his cheeks. Danny punched himself in the thigh, but the tears kept coming.

He stopped at the corner of his street and leaned hard on his crutches. Despite the colorful holiday decorations bedecking every house and the perpetual Christmas carols on the wind, the world felt gray and drab. He'd lost everything, everything that had meant something to him since he was ten years old.

Yeah, things had been off between him and Star for a little while, but Danny would 100 percent rewind the night if he could. He'd go back to before the arcade, when he was just an ignorant guy who had no idea Star was kissing Phil

Waterston on the side. He could live with that, if it meant he still had some semblance of normalcy. He'd already lost basketball; he couldn't stand losing Star right now, too. This whole thing was a nightmare, and it was time to wake up.

Squeezing his eyes tight, he lifted his face to the sky and made a wish—a Christmas wish. Something he never did, but these were desperate times. He counted to three, slowly opened his eyes, and glanced down. His leg was still in a cast, his open toe protected by a red and green striped stocking.

This town was good for nothing.

· · ·

With the entire Page clan currently living under one roof, it wasn't hard to see why Holly's parents had stopped coming here for Christmas years ago.

Grandma's house was like a sardine tin. Holly had nowhere to go, nowhere to hide.

Holly's Vermont aunt and uncle (Vixi and Bob) spent most of their time lying on the couch watching Fox News, dressed in baggy blue jeans and matching plaid flannels, while their gaggle of young kids ran wild through Grandma's living and dining rooms. Holly's eyes were stuck in a permanent eye-roll every time she encountered them. Elda's parents, Donder and Pilar Page, had snapped up Grandma's bedroom off the back of the house and held court in the kitchen most of the time. Holly's own parents, Rudolph (Dolph) and Linda, had commandeered the second floor with R.J., Holly's little brother. Holly and Elda were sharing the attic, which was awesome, because Elda was awesome, except for the part where she kept chatting on the phone with people from home.

This afternoon she was FaceTiming with some guy she'd met in college. Holly adored her cousin, but this dude was well below her station, and Elda totally didn't see it. Teddy was a short, stocky dude who rocked a limp, scraggly comb-over at age twenty-one, and he was playing Elda like a fiddle.

Today Teddy was full-on trying to break up with Elda. He kept mentioning how busy he was and how he was going into his final semester of college and needed to focus. He even managed to mention some girl named "Kara" at three different points during the conversation.

Holly didn't have a ton of dating experience, but she was well-versed in the art of rejection, having been on the receiving end more than a few times. Elda needed to save face here. She couldn't cede the upper hand to this classless jerk-store who treated Elda like garbage. Holly wrote a note on a blank page in her sketch pad and ripped it out.

Carefully avoiding Elda's phone screen, Holly crawled over to the pullout couch the two of them were sharing while in North Pole. She slithered along the floor and reached up to hand Elda the paper. Elda glanced at it and then looked at Holly, mouthing, "What?"

"Tell him." Holly mouthed before crawling back over to the far corner of the attic, where she'd been sorting through her grandparents' old books and magazines in preparation for the family to sell the house.

As Holly pulled open the bottom drawer of a tall, black file cabinet, Elda said, "Teddy, I'm so glad you're saying this. I'm really busy, too, and I could totally use some space. Maybe we should take a break. I don't want to be tied down here in Minnesota. You see, I met someone at the coffee shop—"

Teddy's voice jumped an octave. "Elda, no—" He had obviously planned on being the dumper, but now Elda and Holly had snatched that away from him.

Holly's smile of pride faded away as she peered into the drawer she'd just opened. About a hundred old *National Geographic* magazines were in there. Why had her grandparents bothered saving these? She glanced around the attic, which was full of garbage, basically. Why had they bothered saving any of this?

Her heart ached for her grandma, whose entire life was now on display. Holly made a vow that she would always keep her own house tidy and cleaned out. She'd never want her family members to have to sort through so much junk. She certainly didn't want to leave anything gross or embarrassing hiding in a drawer for her father to find—like he'd found a set of his mother's dentures tucked inside a jewelry box in her nightstand. Her grandmother would have been mortified.

Grandma had died only a few weeks ago, just this past Thanksgiving, while lying on a chaise by Uncle Don's pool in San Diego. She'd had a Moscow Mule in one hand and a pair of sunglasses in the other. Elda's parents had buried Grandma in California, for convenience. The entire family had been there, but it had been a small service. Holly's grandmother had deserved a bigger sendoff. Her life was worth more than an intimate ceremony in a strange place.

There had to be something more they could do to honor her memory.

Elda knelt down next to Holly and wrapped her up in a big hug. "Thank you!" she squealed. Holly hadn't even realized she'd gotten off the phone.

"For what?"

"I told Teddy I needed space, and then he said he wants to get together when we're both back in town. He's going to call me tonight, too." She squeezed Holly tighter, then let go.

"So, you're still going to go out with him?"

"Of course." Elda brushed her hair off her face. She reminded Holly of a girl from a deodorant commercial, all fresh, clean beauty with a baby powder scent. Teddy was the before picture in a gym ad. "He's a total catch, Holly, super smart. He's president of the Young Republicans group on campus. And, obviously, he's hot."

Beauty really must be in the eye of the beholder.

Elda put her hands on Holly's shoulders. "You and I really are an unstoppable team."

Holly's mom yelled up the stairs. "Girls! We're going to dinner in a half hour!"

"Not another family dinner." They'd eaten every meal together since the whole family arrived in North Pole a few days ago. Holly hadn't had two minutes alone to rest and recharge.

Elda shrugged. "Tell your mom you're sick or something."

"Good idea," Holly said.

Elda grinned. "Now I'm the one giving you advice."

Holly's parents let her off the hook for dinner, and she pretended to be napping until she heard the front door slam shut and the car engines turn over in the driveway. Then she jumped out of bed and listened. Holly heard nothing, no sound except the ancient furnace growling in the basement. She was alone. Finally.

She glanced around the attic, suddenly wondering what to do with herself. Holly wouldn't squander this precious time alone. She could read a book or watch TV or just…exist.

Grabbing the biography of the Mitford sisters, Holly dashed downstairs to the kitchen. She snuck a heaping bowl of potato chips and retreated into her grandma's study where they used to plan their gingerbread houses. Grandma would perch on the couch with her knitting, and Holly would sit behind the desk with her sketch pad and pencils.

She took Grandma's spot on the couch and glanced out the window and right into the neighbor's kitchen. A woman stirred a pot on the stove, while a boy sat at the table. A boy with beautiful sandy brown hair and perfect lips.

Holly slid off the couch and onto the floor, ducking out of sight. Danny Garland lived next door? When had that happened? Why had her grandmother never told her?

She crawled along the floor, pulled herself up to a crouch at the windowsill, and peered over at Danny from behind Grandma's green curtain sheers. He tapped away on his phone, glowering. His crutches were propped up next to him, resting against the table.

Grandma'd probably never said anything because she had no idea this news would matter to Holly. She'd had no clue that Holly had been dreaming about Danny since she was ten.

Still, this felt like a sign, like Grandma was reaching to her from beyond the grave. Danny Garland lived next door.

Bah. Stop it, Holly. This was no sign, and, besides, she wasn't supposed to be thinking about Danny Garland anymore. He didn't remember her, and he had a girlfriend. He was off the market, a pipe dream.

His mom put a plate down in front of him, and he pushed it away. He muttered something, and she pointed to the dish, as if trying to get him to eat; then he folded his arms, and she left the room. Danny sat alone after that, staring at the wall in front of him.

Holly boosted herself into the rolling desk chair and whirled toward the window. He looked so sad and angry. Maybe he'd just broken up with his girlfriend. Maybe he needed a friend…

Ugh. Holly's imagination could be so overactive sometimes. She swiveled away from the window, giving Danny some privacy to deal with whatever he was dealing with.

Something gold on the desk caught her eye—embossed lettering scrawled over a red leather book. Her grandmother's name: Dolores Page. She picked up the book and opened it. It was a calendar, but her grandma had used it as a journal and a scrapbook, filling it with little notes and pictures.

Holly glanced around, as if someone might yell at her for

looking at this. But privacy no longer mattered. Grandma's entire life was exposed—her underwear, her dentures, the fact that she'd been hoarding magazines since 1972—what did it matter if Holly peeked inside her day planner?

Her grandmother had scribbled notes and added pictures chronicling the whole year. She'd been to a wedding in town this summer—Matthew and Hakeem's. Judging by a picture of the wedding party, it had been super fancy, too. Holly grinned. Her grandma had been to a gay wedding and Holly'd had no clue. Her grandma had never mentioned it, which probably meant she'd thought it was no big deal. Holly snapped a picture of the page and sent it to her best friend, Rebel, who would totally appreciate it.

A tear splashed on the page, and Holly wiped it away, smearing the ink a bit. Holly brushed away another tear before it could fall. This wasn't sad. It was happy and beautiful. This journal was her grandma in book form.

Holly wasn't sure what she was going to do with it, but she tucked the day planner under her arm and whisked it up to the attic, where she hid it in her suitcase. The others could have the dentures. This book was for her eyes only.

Chapter Three

It'd been a while since Danny had simply watched a basketball game. For the past eight years, he'd always been the one playing. Even while resting on the bench, his mind prepped for his next minutes on the court.

But today he sat in the stands. Brian had driven him out to Countryside High School, about twenty minutes from North Pole. It was an act of bravery and defiance. Phil and Star would be there, and Danny had to reclaim his position with the team. No, he couldn't play, but he could sit on the bench, helping his coach make decisions, passing on his observations about their opponent and how his teammates might adjust. He'd be useful. He'd participate. He'd prove that his usefulness stretched far beyond his ability to shoot a basketball.

But his coach had patted him on the arm and said, "We've got to learn to win without you, Danny."

So he sent Danny back to the stands with his brother,

where he had a full view of Star dancing with the poms squad and Phil Waterston sitting next to the coach, wrapping knees, handing out water bottles, participating in the huddle during timeouts. Watching everyone—his girlfriend, her new boyfriend, Danny's teammates—go on with their lives without him, Danny felt like a fly on the wall at his own funeral.

From the opening tipoff until halftime, Danny was on the verge of tearing his hair out. Star performed dance routines in the corner and snuck little waves at Phil, like she used to do for Danny. His teammates kept making stupid errors. The other team was bigger and faster than the North Pole guys, and the Reindeer were just trying to keep up.

"They should be trying to slow it down," Danny told Brian. "Why are they letting the other team control the pace?"

"We're winning," his brother said.

"For now." Danny folded his arms and frowned. Kevin had taken over Danny's position, power forward, and he'd made some of the dumbest plays on the court. He fouled the other team's center for literally no reason. He tossed the ball up every time it touched his hands, whether he had a decent shot or not. And the one time he tried to pass it, he heaved it out of bounds. Yes, his points were in double digits, but that was pure luck. He put up so many shots, a few were bound to go in. "Kevin is a disaster."

"Kevin is doing fine," Brian said.

When the buzzer rang at the half, the Reindeer were up by five, and the guys all patted each other's backs as they retreated to the locker room. Phil Waterston waved to Star, and she blew him a kiss. Well, that was a new one. Star had never, ever, *ever* blown Danny a kiss, not one time in the six years they were together. She wasn't the kiss-blowing type.

Brian stood. "You want something to drink?"

"Sure." Brian left Danny in the stands, alone and vulnerable to conversations with his teammates' parents. Danny had no desire to make small talk. They'd just want to talk about the game and his leg. Coming here had been a huge mistake.

He pulled out his phone and pretended to play around on it while he watched Star lead the poms squad in a dance to "Jingle Bell Rock" at half court. His eyes met hers for a moment, for the first time all game, and she waved at Danny like they were old friends, like he hadn't just caught her cheating on him last night. Screw that. His eyes jumped back to his phone. They weren't friends. They were nothing. Danny was fine. Totally and completely fine.

He was a survivor, able to adapt to any situation. In fourth grade, he'd joined a park district team with a bunch of his classmates. He'd shown up for the first practice having no clue how to play basketball. He could barely even dribble, because he'd had no one to teach him. His dad had left them when Danny was young, and his mom never cared about sports. Danny had tried asking Brian once, but he just hurled a ball at Danny's head and told him to get lost. So while other guys were out at the park playing sports, Danny stayed home with his mom building LEGOs and doing science experiments.

But Danny put in his time practicing, and somewhere around the fifth game of the season, Danny made his first basket ever. He'd improbably caught a pass and heaved it into the net. It was a total fluke, but everyone clapped and hooted and hollered. Danny knew that feeling of pride. It was the same way he'd always felt after winning the gingerbread competition.

But after the game, another kid told him that Kevin had said Danny was "bad." He was "bad" at basketball. Danny, who'd won every gingerbread contest he'd ever entered, who had read *The Hobbit* when he was seven, had never been "bad" at anything in his life.

He was not going to be "bad" at basketball.

He started going to the park alone to practice. He watched old games on ESPN Classic. He studied famous players' routines and stories. He lived and breathed basketball.

And he made the transition from "bad" to "amazing."

Suddenly Danny started getting invited over by the coolest boys in his grade, including Kevin. Before basketball, the guys would have secret birthday parties and not include Danny. Now he got all the invites.

He abandoned his old life. He stopped entering the gingerbread contest, he quit science club, and he sold all his LEGO sets. Star's best friend, Carolee, cornered Danny at his locker in seventh grade and told Danny that Star wanted him to ask her out. Star was the most beautiful and popular girl in his class. Danny had achieved the adolescent dream— fame, popularity, perfect girlfriend.

Until he made one stupid dunk and ruined everything.

Danny watched as the team filed back out of the locker room. His status had been an illusion. He'd thought he meant more to his team, but here he was relegated to the stands. He'd thought Star had cared about him, but now, watching her act all cute and lovey-dovey with Phil, it was obvious she'd never felt the same way about Danny. The contrast nearly blinded him. She *liked* Phil. She never liked Danny, and he'd been totally oblivious. He'd bent over backward for years to make Star happy; he'd tried so hard to be the kind of guy she wanted him to be.

He couldn't change his leg situation or the fact that Star was with Phil now, but Danny could avoid making the same mistake again. He'd never jump into something because the girl was hot or popular. He'd stop wasting his time pursuing any girl who obviously didn't like him for him.

Danny would never date another Star.

· · ·

On Sunday afternoon, Holly trudged upstairs, toweling off her wet hair. With so many people currently living under the same roof, it was the first time she'd been able to squeeze in a shower all day. She found Elda up in the attic, where she'd thrown herself sideways across the hide-a-bed and buried her face in a pillow, sobbing.

"Oh my God, Elda." Holly, in her robe and slippers, perched next to her cousin's feet and patted an ankle. "What happened?"

Elda heaved herself up to a sitting position. Tears had moistened her face, which only gave her a dewy glow. Elda didn't cry like normal humans. Her skin wasn't blotchy. Her eyes weren't red. "He dumped me. Teddy dumped me."

"Oh." Holly searched for the right words. She hated to see Elda sad, but Teddy wasn't worth the tears. It might take Elda a while to come to that realization herself, but she'd get there eventually. "I'm so sorry. Are you okay?"

"He called me this morning and officially broke it off. He wants to go out with Kara. *Kara*!" Elda wiped her eyes. "Why am I so bad at this? My relationships never last longer than a minute."

At least Elda had gotten the chance to be in a bad relationship. Holly, who liked to think that she understood how the whole game worked, never even got that far. "I don't know, Elda. Maybe you're just going after the wrong guys."

"No." Elda straightened. "It's me. I always ruin things. I'm just, ugh! I always say the wrong thing. Remember how I talked about a freaking dead squirrel with Danny at the coffee shop?" Elda shook out her shoulders. "Everything sucks right now. I need to stop thinking about this."

"Maybe you need to find a guy who's not scared of a little carcass chatter?"

"Yeah, right. That guy doesn't exist. What I need is a better filter, or any filter at all."

"I think I have something to take your mind off guys." Holly got up and went to her suitcase, from which she pulled out her grandma's day planner. Elda needed to see the book more than Holly needed to hide it. "I found this." She handed it to Elda and sat next to her on the pull out couch.

"Is this Grandma's?" Elda started flipping through it. "It's her journal. Oh my God, so cool." Elda stopped on one of the last pages of the calendar, the entries for this week, the one leading up to Christmas. "Aw. She was supposed to go to a holiday dance tonight."

The calendar had been filled through December 31, which was sad and romantic and morbid all at once. Grandma'd had no clue that she wouldn't make it to the end of the year. She'd gone about her business, making appointments and scheduling events. Holly couldn't stop thinking about the impermanence of life. One minute you're here, and the next? Gone.

"She has a date," Elda said. "Frank."

That had been another discovery, thanks to the journal. Grandma'd had a "friend," a guy named Frank, whom she went out with regularly. They were supposed to go together to this dance tonight. "Poor Frank," Holly said. "I had no idea he existed."

"Me neither." Elda flipped to the end of the book. "I wonder if our dads knew?"

Holly giggled. "Probably not. Could you imagine Grandma talking to them about her new boyfriend?"

"They had to assume she'd been dating. Grandpa's been dead for fifteen years." Elda closed the book and ran her hands over the embossed lettering on the cover. "We should go to the dance."

"What? No." Holly'd planned on making a collage out

of the journal, or some kind of word art. She'd never for a second considered actually doing the things in Grandma's calendar. Doing things was not in her comfort zone.

"We totally should. To honor Grandma's memory. We should go meet Frank for this dance and—" Elda flipped open the book to the current page again. "Look, she'd been planning on entering the gingerbread contest. We should do that, too, for old time's sake."

Holly ran her fingers over the words. "Gingerbread contest starts" was scrawled over tomorrow's page in green pen. "I don't think we'll have time. We're supposed to be cleaning out the house." The gingerbread competition and Danny Garland were inextricably tied together in Holly's mind. One did not exist without the other. And Holly was supposed to be forgetting about Danny Garland right now.

"Whatever, *time*," Elda said. "This is our last Christmas in North Pole. We have to do all the things. You know what Grandma told me when she was in L.A. for Thanksgiving?"

Elda had gotten to have one last holiday with Grandma. Holly hadn't. She could hardly remember last summer, when Grandma had come down to Chicago for a week. What had they even talked about? Why hadn't Holly asked Grandma what she'd been up to? Why hadn't Grandma told her about the wedding she'd gone to a few weeks before? Maybe it had been Holly's fault because she hadn't asked, because she'd been too busy with her sculpting and hanging out with friends and working at the Chicken Shack. Now she'd never have the chance to get those answers.

"Grandma said she was sad that you and I and the other grandkids had grown apart, that we didn't know each other how we used to when we were younger," Elda said. "Like, remember when we dressed R.J. and my brother up as girls and took them to the park because we wanted sisters?"

"I totally forgot about that. I bet R.J. has no memory

of it." Holly grinned as the memories came flooding back. She remembered the time R.J. sat in an anthill and had ants running from his diaper down his legs. Or when they'd play murder mystery in Grandma's den, using old Halloween costumes and toy weapons.

"I have the receipts," Elda said. "We took pictures of our sweet little 'sisters,' Roberta and Sally. I keep them locked in my room and trot them out any time Sal brings home a new girlfriend. Usually it backfires, though. He's proud of how his legs look in a skirt. Anyway, I'll send you copies."

Holly laughed. "I'd love to see those." She took the book back from Elda. It was heavy in her hands, and the pages were soft from use. Holly stared at tonight's entry: *Holiday Dance, Town Hall, Frank.* Grandma had drawn a heart next to his name. "Maybe we should go to this dance," she said. "For Grandma."

"Yes!" Elda jumped off the pull out couch, and the springs under the mattress creaked. "For Grandma."

Giggling, Holly and Elda ran downstairs and raided Grandma's closet, which was still full of vintage dresses from the '70s and '80s. When they were kids, she and Elda used to try on these frocks and then perform elaborate plays for their parents down in the living room. The musty scent of Grandma's old clothes transported Holly back in time. Everything came back to her—the songs they used to sing, the choreographed dances to Elvis's entire catalog, how her mom and dad used to cuddle on the couch laughing while Holly and Elda danced.

When Holly and Elda went downstairs to find dresses for the Christmas gala, a few of their younger cousins followed them into Grandma's room and started rummaging through all the old clothes and jewelry. The little kids had never seen this stuff before. And tonight, they made plans to put on dresses and sing for their parents. Life was cyclical.

"The wigs!" Elda squealed, pulling open one of Grandma's drawers. "I've been wanting to get my hands on these forever."

Their grandma used to wear wigs whenever she had to dress up. Holly's dad had maintained she'd just liked changing up her look from time to time, but that explanation was way too boring. "I used to think she was a spy, like on *The Americans*."

Elda raised an eyebrow. "Who's to say she wasn't?" She plopped a blond wig on top of her head. Her long, brown locks flowed out from under the golden pixie cut, giving her a glorious two-toned mullet. "This is totally me, right?"

"Oh, for sure." Holly grabbed a black bob with bangs that actually stayed put, unlike her real hair. "What if I started wearing this all the time, if I just showed up back home with a wig and didn't say anything. Would anyone notice?"

"You look hot," Elda said. "You should do it. Just start rocking the wig, like 'This is me, take it or leave it.'"

Holly stared at herself in the mirror, running her tongue along the back of her scar again. She did look hot. She looked tough and put-together. "Let's pick our dresses." She grabbed one she remembered from when she was a kid—a strapless black and gold dress with a sweetheart neckline she used to call the "Wicked Snow White" dress. She pulled it over her clothes and zipped it up with a silent prayer. It fit. It was an actual North Pole miracle.

Elda had stripped down to her underwear, because she had a figure like a bikini model, and pulled on a kelly green dress with long, lacy sleeves and a pleated, floor-length skirt. "Grandma wore this to her little sister's wedding in, like, 1979. Bridesmaid dress. I remember the pictures." She put her arm around Holly, and they posed together in the mirror. "Almost perfect."

They did their makeup—going for full, bold, Urban

Decay glam. Elda hid her real hair under the short, blond wig, and Holly stripped off her robe (alone, in the privacy of the bathroom) and put on the dress. They found fancy capes and major platform heels in Grandma's closet. Their grandma may or may not have been a spy, but tonight Holly and Elda were. They were going incognito to North Pole's fanciest ball.

On the sidewalk outside Grandma's house, Elda twirled as Holly fixed her cape around her shoulders. She glanced over at Danny's house. It was mostly dark, save for a few lights in the back of the house.

As if reading Holly's mind, Elda said, "I wonder if we'll meet any hot guys at the dance tonight."

"Maybe," Holly said. Though Danny Garland might not be among them. Those crutches weren't very conducive to dancing. He was probably sitting home alone thinking about his gingerbread showstopper entry or reading a book or watching some really interesting documentary about history or architecture. Holly liked to picture him doing those things sans girlfriend, which was naive. He and this girlfriend were probably together all the time, doing all the things they loved to do together. She was probably an amazing gingerbread house builder.

"Maybe we can team up tonight," Elda said. "I can lure the guys over to us, because that's where I really shine. Then you can keep me from saying words like 'toe jam' or 'deer scat' once the conversation gets going."

Holly grinned. "I think I can handle that. If I kick you in the shins, it means stop talking about blood and guts and hairballs."

Elda fixed the strap on her platform sandal. "And if I kick *you* in the shins, it means loosen up and smile at whatever cute guy is grooving on you."

"What are you talking about? I smile all the time!" Holly

had never had anyone tell her to lighten up and smile more. Okay, except for her BFF Rebel sometimes. And her parents. And freaking R.J., but what did he know? Holly didn't have to smile just to make other people feel more comfortable. She was allowed to wear any facial expression she pleased.

"You don't smile," came a voice from the porch behind the girls. Holly swung around. Her cousin Sal, Elda's brother, stood there, all dressed up like he was going to the dance, too. "Remember when you were in town for the funeral and I introduced you to my friend Patrick?"

Holly shrugged. "I don't know. Maybe." She didn't remember a Patrick. She'd met a lot of people that day.

"He thought you were hot, so I arranged a meeting." Sal adjusted the cuffs on his button-down shirt. "But you were, like, totally aloof and acted like you wanted nothing to do with him."

He had to be kidding with this. "I was at my grandma's funeral, Sal. What did he expect? Little Miss Sunshine?"

"I don't know, man," Sal said. "He thought you were mean."

Rolling her eyes, Holly turned to Elda. "Tell your brother I'm not mean."

Elda wrapped an arm around Holly. "You're not mean. You're tough and strong and opinionated. Those are good qualities." She squeezed Holly's shoulder. "But friendliness is okay, too, you know. Maybe loosen up tonight. Be open to new people, new experiences. I'll be there to help you, okay? I'm your wingwoman, too."

"You two are losers." Sal brushed past the girls and headed down the street.

"Why don't you put on a skirt, Sal? Show off your legs a little?" Holly yelled after him.

He responded by flipping her two birds.

Laughing, Holly said, "I miss this, Elda. I love that we're

all hanging out again."

"Me, too." She pulled Holly into a hug. "Let's never lose touch again. Promise? Friends forever?"

"Friends forever," Holly said.

Chapter Four

Danny's mom forced him to go to the mayor's annual Christmas ball. It was a North Pole tradition, and everyone in town always went, but Danny should've gotten a pass this year, what with his crutches and the fact that he'd just been dumped. He did not.

"You're going," his mom had said as she put on dangly emerald green earrings. "It'll be a good distraction. What would you do otherwise? Stay here and play video games?"

Yes, that was what he'd do. Maybe video games were his new purpose in life.

"Maybe you'll meet someone." His mom waggled her eyebrows.

"Mom, I just broke up with Star." And he didn't trust his judgment. Or his ability to talk to girls. Every time he thought about meeting the two cute girls in Santabucks the other day and how he'd completely blown it with both of them, Danny's whole body shuddered involuntarily. He was a total dork trapped inside a hot guy's body. He would be single for the rest of his life.

At the dance, Danny perched himself at a table near the DJ booth, where Craig spun the Christmas tunes.

"Nice suit." Craig pressed a few keys on his computer like he was the most important person in the room and his DJ-ing abilities were going to solve world hunger or something.

"Thanks." Danny sipped non-alcoholic eggnog and tried hard not to watch Star and Phil dancing together in the middle of their circle of friends. *Thanks a bunch, Mom.*

"You look like an eight-year-old about to make his First Communion," Craig said.

"Are you a fashion critic now?" Danny didn't tell Craig that he looked like a stereotypical nerd, what with his hiked-up mom jeans and suspenders over a geeky *Game of Thrones*-themed Christmas T-shirt, because nerdy was the aesthetic Craig strived for. It was completely and utterly *him*. Danny was the one wearing a costume tonight. Danny was the one pretending to enjoy himself while being forced to watch his ex-girlfriend nuzzle her cheek against her new boyfriend's neck.

"You should go dance." Craig flipped to some Mariah Carey song from one of her Christmas albums and everyone in the crowd whooped with glee. Mariah was big around these parts.

This lousy, predictable town. "Crutches, Craig. Remember? You tried to keep me out of the laser tag room last night?"

"Yeah, so why are you being such a wimp now?" He feigned crying, rubbing his fists over his eyes. "'Boo-hoo! My leg is broken and I'm sad.'"

Danny's brother Brian came over with a small, unfamiliar blonde on his arm. Danny had never been so happy to see his brother and one of his flavors of the week. Anyone would be better than Craig at this point.

But then Brian said, "You should get out there and

dance."

Traitor.

"That's what I told him." Craig rammed a toothpick into one of the cocktail wieners he'd managed to get Dinesh to procure for him.

"Crutches. Cast." Danny waved an arm toward his leg. "Also"—he pointed to his chest—"recently dumped."

Brian waved him off. "All the more reason to get out there and work the floor. The Page girls are here." Brian nodded toward the far corner of the room, where two girls in silly dresses and obvious wigs were heading toward the refreshments.

"The Page girls?" Danny asked.

"Mrs. Page's granddaughters. They're in town going through her stuff."

Danny hadn't noticed anyone over at Mrs. Page's house, but then he hadn't been paying attention. "She was always talking about her granddaughters." His neighbor had been trying to set Danny up with one of them for years, but they never came back to visit, plus he'd been with Star the whole time.

"Yeah," Brian said. "And they're hot."

The girls turned around, and it was like a spotlight landed on their faces. These were the girls from the coffee shop. "Oh, shit." He ducked his head down and tried to cover his face.

"What?" Brian said.

"I know them. They came into Santabucks yesterday, and I was a total mess."

"What did you do?" Now Craig leaned toward Danny and Brian, trying to butt into this conversation, because he was obviously so skilled with the ladies and had much wisdom to impart. Whatever, *Craig*.

"I don't know." Danny's face warmed just thinking about

it. "I thought one of them was flirting with me, so I blurted out that I had a girlfriend, and then the other one kind of looked at me like I was a weirdo."

"Well, you don't have a girlfriend anymore," Brian said.

"And you are a weirdo," Craig added.

"Thanks, guys." Danny spotted Star on the dance floor with Phil, the two of them having a great time together, spinning across the floor like tops.

"You should go over and apologize for being a little off yesterday," Brian said. "Tell them you were going through a breakup, and you didn't know what you were saying, something like that."

"Let them see how sad you are," Craig said. "Girls love a wounded guy. They'll want to help you. Seduction 101."

Danny blinked at Craig. "What do you know about seduction?"

"I've seen a lot of movies."

The girls were over by Frank from the hardware store now, talking and laughing with him and Nancy, who owned the bakery. The Page girls were both, objectively, really good looking. Now that he thought about it, he vaguely remembered them as kids, when they all used to enter the gingerbread contest. They'd been twins, almost, with their long, skinny legs and brown hair. He hadn't been able to tell them apart back then. They were just Mrs. Page's granddaughters. Interchangeable.

But now he'd definitely noticed them, and they were only going to be in town for a short time. Yeah, he'd made a bad first impression at the coffee shop, but circumstances had changed. He was single now. It was time for him to get out there and start learning how to flirt. These girls, tourists with whom he had a shared history, would be a good start. They'd be like the training wheels on his bicycle of being single.

Danny grabbed his crutches and stood. Craig started a

one-man cheer of "Danny, Danny, Danny!"

"Shhh!" Danny hissed. He maneuvered himself across the room, like he was trying to find an open hole on the basketball court—bobbing and weaving his way through people dancing and balloons and streamers littering the floor.

He slid to a stop right behind the girls, swaying a little as his crutches stopped before he did.

Frank waved. "Danny!"

"Hi, Frank."

The girls swung around.

"Oh, hey," Danny said, feigning surprise at seeing them at the dance. That's what flirting was all about, right? Pretending to have other things going on in your life besides trying to snag the attention of a desirable human being? "We met at Santabucks the other day."

The taller one, the one in the blond wig, grinned right at him. Her teeth, which had been hidden behind full lips, were perfect, straight and white. She was a living, breathing pop-up ad. She was the kind of girl who could convince a guy he needed skinny jeans even when he most definitely did not. "We remember," she said.

"You seemed unimpressed by my cousin's thoughts on dead squirrels." The shorter one had a harder edge to her, which kind of terrified Danny, honestly, but in a way that intrigued him. She kept looking at him like he hadn't fooled her. It was how Star used to look at him, like he had to earn her respect and admiration.

Something that was not like Star? This girl had a tattoo of a puppy on her collarbone. A puppy, not a skull or a dragon or something else that was cheesily hardcore. A puppy. That made it even more punk rock, for some reason. This girl would eat Danny alive. She nodded toward her taller cousin. "Elda's always using the animal carcass line on guys. It's like a personality test. If you bolt, you're no fun. If you laugh at the joke, we know you're cool. If you come off way too interested, we cut and run."

"You bolted." Elda raised an eyebrow.

"I had a girlfriend," Danny reminded her.

"Had?" the shorter one asked.

The whole situation still felt surreal. Danny was single now. He was talking to two girls he might want to ask out. "We broke up. Last night."

The shorter one folded her arms and frowned at him, unimpressed.

Danny focused on Elda, who actually seemed to welcome his presence. "My brother tells me you're Mrs. Page's granddaughters."

"Elda." She offered him a perfect, slender hand with pointy, gunmetal nails. "And this is Holly. My cousin."

Holly gave Danny a bored little half-nod as her eyes followed Frank, who had wandered off to talk to someone else.

"You two used to do the gingerbread contest," Danny said. They were his biggest competition, and once they stopped coming to North Pole, Danny stopped entering the contest.

"Yes, we did." Elda beamed at him. The lights glinted off her white teeth.

"You kicked our ass every year." Holly's voice was soft. She'd dropped the death glare and grinned at him now. God, she was cute when she smiled. More than that, Danny felt like he'd earned something. Her top lip was slightly crooked thanks to a scar that bisected the divot between her nose and lip. What was that called again...? "Philtrum," he said out loud. Then he covered his mouth. He'd actually blurted that out. Smooth, Dan.

"What?" Elda said.

Holly blushed and put a hand to her mouth. She knew

exactly what he was talking about. "Street fight," she said, dropping her hand. "Bad habit." He could see the motion of her tongue running along the back of the scar.

He narrowed his eyes at her. She wasn't for real, obviously. She was playing with him, being mysterious. Well, two could play at that game. He gave her a slow smile and nodded to his leg. "I gave up my *Mortal Kombat* days too late, myself."

Holly opened her mouth to reply, but Elda cut in. "You two are goofy. You doing the gingerbread contest this year?"

"I don't know." Danny hadn't thought about it. He hadn't competed in years, because he never wanted to. But he had absolutely nothing else going on right now. "Maybe."

"We are." Elda did a little hop, then nudged Holly in the ribs.

"I found Grandma's day planner, and Elda and I are doing everything on her calendar through the end of the year." Holly nabbed a cup of eggnog from a passing waiter. "Our parents are selling the house, so this is our last time in North Pole. We're knocking everything off our bucket list." Holly looked off to the side as if hunting for someone better to talk to. She did not like Danny, that much was obvious. She probably thought he was an ass for flirting with her and her cousin yesterday while he still had a girlfriend. Well, that was no longer the case. Flirting was totally legal now.

"Your grandma," he said, his heart pounding in his chest, "she was always threatening to set me up with one of you, the one with the gingerbread skills." Danny had been with the same girl for six years. This was the closest he'd come to making a move since he was eleven.

"Elda," Holly said right away. She draped her arm across her cousin's shoulders. "Elda's the gingerbread queen."

Damn. Apparently he'd already made up his mind about which Page girl he wanted to be with, and it wasn't Elda. Danny tried hard not to let the disappointment show. He was being stupid, repeating old patterns, because he obviously had this weird need to be liked by everyone, especially girls who wanted nothing to do with him. Elda had been smiling at him throughout this entire conversation. Elda did not hate his guts. The logical move here was to pursue her, not Holly. If Elda was the one his neighbor had wanted to set him up with, she probably had a good reason for it. "Maybe the two of us should get together some time to talk strategy."

Elda hooked her arm through Holly's. "Only if my cousin can come, too. We're partners."

"Sure." He mentally tried to murder all the butterflies that had popped up in his stomach at the thought of hanging out with Holly. "Bring your A game, though. I'm looking for a challenge this year."

. . .

"God, that was so fun!" Elda dashed down Main Street, Grandma's velvet cape fluttering behind her like a superhero costume. She spun around and waited for Holly to catch up. "I needed that, for real." She put her hands on her hips. "But why did you say what you said?"

"What do you mean?" Holly pulled her own cape tighter around her torso. It still wasn't normal Minnesota freezing, but it was definitely chilly. Even the sweat Holly had worked up on the dance floor had stopped warming her.

"You told Danny I was good at building gingerbread houses. You know that's not true. You're the gingerbread queen."

"Yeah, but I don't want him." Holly's throat had been dry the whole night. She'd written him off after The Coffee Shop Incident because he'd said he had a girlfriend. But now he didn't. The reason for her not doing the terrifying thing and confessing how she'd felt about him for years was gone. Now her only excuse was Elda. "You like him, right?"

"He's super cute."

"Then we're going to put our combined superpowers to the test." She pointed to herself and then to Elda. "We are going to make Danny Garland fall hopelessly in love with you."

Elda narrowed her eyes for a moment as if figuring out the logic of this, then a slow, massive smile crept across her face. "You're gonna keep me from being a total goober!"

"Yes," Holly said. "I'm going make sure you avoid any mention of roadkill in your effort to seduce him."

Elda rubbed her arms for warmth. The Christmas lights bounced off the ten or so rings she was wearing on both hands. "I see one potential problem with this."

Just one? "What's that?"

"Danny seemed to think that Grandma wanted to set him up with the granddaughter who used to enter the gingerbread contest with her. That'd be you." Elda pointed to her chest and shook her head. "Not me."

"You were part of the team, too, Elda. Grandma could've easily meant you." Though Danny had said "the one with the gingerbread skills." Grandma would have definitely meant Holly, not Elda. But Grandma saw all of her grandchildren as special. Her lack of objectivity had blinded her to the fact that hot, popular guys like Danny didn't go for girls like Holly. Hell, guys like Teddy didn't go for girls like Holly. She was used to it, fine with it. She'd been on this roller coaster a million times.

Danny had obviously been looking at Elda during The Coffee Shop Incident. Holly had seen it firsthand, and it was how things were supposed to be. It was biology. If Holly couldn't have Danny, then she'd help her beautiful, romantically challenged cousin get him. No big deal.

Holly lived a rich and fulfilling life inside her imagination.

It was safe there. She didn't get hurt there. She was friendly and beautiful and no one called her awful names like they did at school. In her dreams, the guys she liked always picked her over her beautiful cousin or any other gorgeous girl in the room.

But whenever she'd tried to take her fantasy into the real world, it had ended in disaster.

She and Danny had a great rapport, but Holly wasn't a fool. She'd been here before. She'd had this friend, Charlie, back at school. The two of them started talking in the middle of freshman year and had gotten so close people assumed they were dating. They sat together in every mutual class. They ate lunch together. They hung out in the hallway before school and scribbled out math assignments together. Holly felt like maybe, *maybe* something was there. Charlie obviously liked her as a person. Even outside of school, he called and texted her. Romance was the next logical step in their relationship.

So, she wrote him a letter expressing her feelings and left it in his locker.

He said nothing.

For three days.

Finally, her best friend Rebel went up to him after school (after Holly'd asked her to) and was like, "Did you get the letter?"

He said yes, the two of them chatted, and Charlie told Rebel the thing he was too chicken to tell Holly to her face: "I don't like her like that, and I never will."

Holly stayed far away from Charlie after that. She'd ruined their friendship. She should've just kept quiet and let things carry on as they had been, because the hope, the dreams, the imagining what could be was always sweeter than the disappointment of reality.

And Holly would not make the same mistake with Danny Garland.

"Can we start walking?" Holly took off down Main Street, toward their grandma's house. The air smelled like cinnamon, and every shop window glowed with lights and tinsel. North Pole at night was exquisite. Nothing else in the world could compare. Holly drew in a long, deep breath, taking in the cold air and the sooty smell of smoke from a hundred different fireplaces.

Elda ran to catch up with Holly, her platform shoes clomping against the cobblestone sidewalk. "You sure you don't like Danny? We never discussed it. I don't want to call dibs."

Holly's breath caught for a moment as she imagined what would happen if she did the unthinkable and told Elda she liked Danny. In her head, she saw herself dancing with Danny and kissing him and hoisting the gingerbread trophy over her head as he clapped with pride. But that wasn't reality. Reality was him telling Elda that he didn't like Holly "like that," and he never would. "No way," Holly said. "He's not my type."

"Really?" Elda said.

"Definitely. I'm a nerd girl, obviously."

"Okay..." The two of them walked in silence for about half a block, then Elda said, "Thank you."

"For what?"

"Can I tell you something?" Elda, who'd been dancing through the streets earlier, seemingly unaffected by the cold, pulled her cape tighter around her arms. "You have to promise not to tell anyone, though."

They passed someone's front lawn, which had been decorated with a gang of motorcycle-riding blowup characters—Santa and Snoopy and Frosty and a whole bunch of others. "I promise. Of course I won't tell."

Elda linked her arm in Holly's. "It's not just the guy stuff that's got me down. I'm dropping out of school."

Holly's feet stopped moving, yanking Elda to a stop.

"What?" Holly said.

The cousins faced each other on the sidewalk. "College isn't for me. I got there and was just like, 'I don't want this. I'm not meant to sit in a classroom.' Is that ridiculous?"

This conversation gave Holly whiplash. They'd gone from Danny Garland to school in a matter of seconds. "I...I don't know what to say." Everyone went to college. At least everyone Holly knew. Her parents expected her to go, and same with all her friends' parents. That was non-negotiable. And Elda was giving up after only one semester. "What do you plan on doing instead?"

Elda frowned. "I don't know. I've been waiting to tell my parents until after this trip, because they have so much on their minds, but they're going to murder me. I thought I'd have everything figured out by now, so I could go to Mom and Dad and be like, 'Here's what I want to do with my life. Here's my plan,' but I've got nothing." She held out her empty hands.

"Wow." This wasn't completely off-brand for her. When they were kids, Elda was always jumping from potential career to potential career—a police officer, a cosmetologist, a dermatologist, a circus performer. Even in the short time since the two of them had gotten closer, Holly had witnessed some of this flightiness. She constantly changed her mind about things—about where to go on spring break or whether or not to dye her hair or what to have for dinner. But leaving college without a plan—that had more repercussions than whether to order Mexican or Chinese.

"You think it's a bad idea," Elda said.

"No..."

"Yes, you do." Elda dropped her head to her hands.

Holly rubbed her cousin's back. "I'm only wondering whether or not you've thought this through."

"I don't know." She lifted her head. "But I know college

is what I don't want, so isn't that enough?"

"Maybe..." Holly was usually so focused on being responsible and doing the right, safe, consequence-free thing that "want" or "not want" never entered the equation.

Elda put an arm around Holly, wrapping her in velvet and their grandmother's old lady perfume. "But let's not think about that now. Let's talk about how the two of us are going to use our superpowers of seduction on Danny Garland."

This felt like a "want" or "not want" situation all of a sudden. Holly wanted Danny, that was for sure. But he kept checking out Elda, and he'd directed his invitation to hang out right at her.

The thing was, the Danny of Holly's imagination couldn't hold a candle to Danny in real life. He was whatever the opposite of a Monet was. Danny was lovely from afar, but exquisite up close. His skin looked like it had been airbrushed. His lips revealed not even a hint of dryness. And he was nice, too. And funny, damn it. And smart. He'd had the world "philtrum" on the tip of his tongue.

When it came right down to it, what Holly really wanted was to be able to see Danny and talk to him. Helping Elda would achieve that. Holly would get to chat with him a bit and hang out. She'd be able to leave North Pole with some great, fun memories. She was only going to be here for two more weeks. It wasn't like she and Danny were ever, in any universe, going to end up together.

She rested her head on Elda's shoulders. "First of all, my sweet coz, less is more. If you feel the need to say something, say nothing. I'll fill in the conversation gaps. You create mystery. Trust me. You and Danny will be madly in love by Christmas Eve." Holly smiled, though that thought had left a sour pit in her stomach.

Chapter Five

Sunday, December 17

"Welcome, everyone, to the start of this year's gingerbread contest!"

Danny only half-heard Mayor Sandoval's announcement. He was too busy making drinks behind the counter. It was North Pole tradition for different stores to host each event in the gingerbread competition, and Danny's mom had offered to arrange the launch, which meant all hands were on deck. Brian and Jamison, one of the Santabucks baristas, were taking orders. Danny and his mom were making drinks. Some of the newer employees were working the floor. It still wasn't enough. The place was packed.

He'd perched behind the espresso machine on a stool, with a chair to keep his leg elevated. He and his mom had figured out quite the system. He made the drinks. She fetched stuff from the fridge and kept the counter stocked. By the time the mayor started talking, almost everyone had gotten their beverages and had settled into their seats.

Star and Phil were at a two-person table near the door. She'd acknowledged Danny with a curt nod and blushed sheepishly as she rattled off her order to Jamison. Star had wanted her usual non-fat, sugar-free vanilla latte, but Danny had "accidentally" given her the full-sugar syrup. Never cheat on the guy who makes your coffee.

The Page girls had come in as well; they sat at a table near the counter. Holly faced away from Danny, arms crossed over her bright red sweater. She'd barely looked at him when she'd come in, but Elda had waved cheerily and kept sneaking glances at Danny every few seconds. Just to see what would happen, Danny shot her a wave from behind the espresso machine, and Elda beamed as if no guy had ever looked her way before. Wow, okay. Maybe he wasn't a complete disaster around women.

His mom nudged him in the side. "What's up with the big smile, Dan?"

"Nothing, Mom. Ugh." She could be so embarrassing.

"As most of you know," the mayor said, "the gingerbread contest is in three parts. Round one is decorating gingerbread people, round two is building and decorating a traditional gingerbread house on site, and round three is the showstopper, which is to be built over the next week and brought to the town hall on Christmas Eve, the final day of the competition."

Despite his initial reservations about entering the contest and his usual aversion to anything Christmassy, Danny had stayed up most of last night thinking about his showstopper. He'd always been the king of the third round, but it had been eight years since he'd last entered the contest. He hadn't even eaten gingerbread since then. Still, he planned on going big for the final round. He'd build a gingerbread replica of a basketball court, complete with gingerbread players. He'd tile the floor in gingerbread glazed with sugar syrup and build the bench and stands. If it turned out half as good as it looked in his imagination, he might have a shot at another blue ribbon.

He was actually excited about a North Pole Christmas event. It was like he'd wandered into a new dimension.

"What are you doing for the showstopper?" he whispered across the counter to Elda.

Her eyes went wide, and she blushed. She opened her mouth to say something, but Holly kicked her under the table. As if remembering herself, Elda put a finger to her lips and pointed to the mayor, who was still talking. Danny turned to watch, even though he knew all this already.

"All materials must be edible, though they may be store bought," Mayor Sandoval was saying. "The structures must stand upright on their own. You may work in teams of no more than two this year."

Danny grinned at the girls. "I don't need a partner." He was always good for some trash talk.

"Neither does Elda. I'm just the eye candy." Holly licked a bit of whipped cream off her straw. She'd ordered the special drink Danny's mom had created for this event—a ginger apple cider. She'd ordered it as advertised, not asking for special non-sugar sugar or unsweetened whipped cream, which Danny respected. This girl could probably wrap herself in literal garbage and he'd find it hot, simply because it made her an "individual." He'd compared her to Star before, but other than the whole "looking at Danny with disdain" thing, Holly and Star were polar opposites. Holly didn't seem to care what other people thought, which was certainly not the case for Star.

He leaned across the counter, making sure to speak directly to Elda, even though he hoped Holly understood this was meant for her, too. "If you ladies want to get together to practice your piping work, you know where to find me." That sounded dirtier than he meant it to. His good knee buckled when Danny realized what he'd just said. He straightened up, pretending not to have noticed the double entendre.

Elda had noticed. She blushed.

"You just want to spy on our showstopper." Holly raised a thick, perfectly arched eyebrow.

"That's absolutely why." He couldn't suppress the smile. He tried, and he failed.

"At least you're honest about it," Holly said with a very slight grin, almost as if she didn't totally despise him.

And that was the best thing to happen to Danny all day.

"Maybe we should exchange numbers." He directed that at Holly. Logically, he should be setting his sights on Elda, but apparently he was a glutton for punishment.

Holly held out her hand. "Give me your phone."

He unlocked it and handed it over, watching as she typed her info into his contacts like a total boss. Holly's hands weren't pristinely manicured like Elda's or Star's. She had short, uneven fingernails. Why? Did she not bother doing her nails because she worked with her hands? Was she in between manicures? Whatever the reason, Danny wanted to know. He needed all the info. He'd opened the book of Holly, and he couldn't put it down.

She handed the phone back, and Danny checked his contacts under "P" for Page. He found an entry for Elda. Not Holly. Elda. Danny's heart sank, but he forced an enthusiastic smile. Even Holly herself was telling him to forget about her and go after Elda. Maybe he should listen.

He grinned at Elda. "I'll text you later."

Again, her face went bright red, and she said nothing. It was like someone had glued her lips shut.

Once the mayor ended his spiel, Danny was back on duty making drinks. Their last customer finally left after nine-fifteen, leaving only Danny, Brian, their mom, and Jamison in the shop to close up.

"I saw you talking to the Page girls," Brian said. He was restocking the fridge while their mom did the receipts and Jamison cleaned the front of the shop. Danny remained on his stool, wiping down the espresso machine and making sure to prep everything for tomorrow. Having a broken leg sucked for many, many reasons, but at least it got him out of sweeping, mopping, and taking out the garbage.

"They seem nice," Danny's mom said.

"They are nice." All the blood in his body rushed to his cheeks. He wasn't sure he'd call Holly "nice," but she was definitely something.

Brian squeezed Danny's shoulder. "And one of them is maybe the hottest girl ever to set foot in North Pole."

Yes, she was.

"You say that about a different girl every season, Brian." Jamison swept some garbage into a dustbin. "Who was it last summer?"

"The gymnast," Danny said.

Their mom looked up from counting fives. "Gymnast? Didn't you like Sam's friend? That Jane girl?"

"Jane and the gymnast were cute," Brian said, "but the Page girl is hot. What's her name, Dan?"

Danny started to say "Holly," but Jamison cut him off. "Which one?" She leaned on her broom, challenging Brian. Jamison and Brian had always bickered like siblings, ever since she started working at the store. "There are two Page girls."

Brian rolled his eyes. "You know which one. Don't be dense."

"I only want you to recognize how big a dick you're being." Jamison glanced at the boys' mother. "Sorry, Maggie."

Maggie Garland shook her head. "I'm on your side. Girls are more than their appearances, boys."

"I know, *Mom*," Danny said. Holly was hot, yes, but she

was more than that.

"All I'm saying is," Jamison said, "don't go after Elda just because you think she's pretty."

"Elda?" Danny asked. Who was talking about Elda?

"Yeah." Jamison said. "I mean, you dated Star."

"And?" Danny had wandered into a completely different conversation from the one he'd thought he was having.

Jamison shrugged. "And Star was—*is*—gorgeous, but she took you for granted, Danny, and she wasn't very nice. I don't want to see you make the same mistake again."

"I don't either." Though that was exactly what he was doing with Holly. She didn't like him. She'd made that clear both by looking at him like she couldn't possibly be more unimpressed and by physically typing her cousin's number into his phone. She'd basically handed him off to another girl, so she obviously didn't want him.

"I'm just saying." Jamison tied up a garbage bag. "Picking the quote-unquote hot Page over the other one, maybe that's just you picking style over substance again."

Brian tossed a wadded-up paper towel at her. "Now you're jumping to conclusions. Just because someone's not hot doesn't mean they're automatically a good, interesting person. And vice versa."

"True, but I'm just saying maybe Danny should get to know these girls before jumping into anything—"

"And I'm just saying maybe he should do whatever the hell he wants because he's single for the first time ever, and also it's a free country."

Danny hopped up from his stool, and Brian handed him his crutches.

"Jamison, it pains me to say this, but Brian's actually right on this one. Sort of," Danny said. "Both Page girls are cool, but Elda's the 'nice' one. Holly—" *Is hot and sexy and frustrating and doesn't like me and would probably end up hurting me like Star did.* "Holly wants absolutely nothing to do with me."

Jamison shook her head. "I don't buy it. I saw you interacting with both of them, and I definitely saw sparks between you and the one with the glasses."

Any sparks, if they existed at all, had come from him. Holly had made her position extremely clear. "I don't know." Danny shrugged. "I've talked to both of them, and Holly looks at me like I'm only slightly less disgusting than gum on the bottom of her shoe. I just got out of a relationship like that, and, frankly, I don't want to do that again."

"Fair enough," Jamison said.

Brian put an arm around his brother. "And you know what? Since you called dibs on the hotter Page, I'll go after the other one."

"You're disgusting," Jamison said.

"You actually are." Danny nudged his brother's arm off his shoulders. Brian was not going to make Holly Page one of his Christmas break conquests.

"I've never claimed otherwise," Brian said.

Danny rolled his eyes hard at Jamison.

"I hope you strike out spectacularly," she said.

"I'm with Jamison," Maggie added.

"I bet she laughs in your face," Danny said. If Danny underwhelmed Holly, Brian Garland was going to physically repulse her. At least that's what Danny was counting on.

Brian held out a hand. "I'll take that bet."

Danny shook his brother's hand, making sure to add an extra-firm squeeze at the end. Holly Page had to say no to his brother. She simply had to.

• • •

Monday, December 18

"This is all new to me," Elda said, rubbing her hands together. "What do we do first?"

Holly sipped her coffee and glanced down Main Street, which buzzed with tourists. Grandma's house was a zoo, but it was nothing compared to downtown North Pole at ten o'clock on a Monday morning the week before Christmas. The girls had stopped in for caffeine at Santabucks, but Danny hadn't been working. His brother, Brian, was there, and he'd written his number on the side of Holly's cup.

"Maybe we can double date," he'd said with a nod toward Elda.

Holly had rolled her eyes so hard she nearly strained a muscle.

That's why the two of them were standing outside on this cold, gray morning, instead of sitting on warm, padded chairs listening to Christmas carols in the coffee shop.

"First we've got to buy the candy." Holly took the tiniest sip of her blazing hot mocha. "Since it's the morning after the gingerbread kickoff party, people are going to be storming the candy shop and grocery store today, grabbing everything they can. We need to fight like hell to get what we need. No mercy." She nodded toward her cousin's hands. "Good thing you've got those nails. We'll need them."

Holly headed down the street toward the candy store. The showstopper was taking shape in her head already. They were going to build a gingerbread model of their grandma's house. It was something she and her grandma had discussed doing once, the year before the Pages stopped coming back to North Pole for Christmas. Since she and Elda were already using Grandma's day planner as a guide for their time in town, they'd channel her brain for the contest. They were going to need gumdrops and licorice whips and some kind of fruit leather for the wooden slats on the outside of the house. Holly hadn't gotten that far yet in her plans, so their best course of action was to simply buy everything they could get their hands on and sort it out later.

"Maybe we *should* double date," Elda said.

"Well, that's a non-sequitur." Holly glanced inside the bakery as they passed the window. She noticed some giant lollipops and fancy cookies on the shelves, plus who knew what else. Holly was open to inspiration. She had some really cool, unorthodox ideas for decorations—like making wrought iron fencing out of dried spaghetti and royal icing, which was something she'd seen on a website and was desperate to try.

"It's not, really," Elda said. "We should all go out—me and Danny and you and his brother."

"Oh. That...no. That's not going to happen." Brian came off as smarmy and kind of dumb. He reminded her of the guys from her neighborhood at home who seemed to believe that knowing their way around a hockey rink counted as enough personality to get them through life. Plus, did Elda really think Holly would go on a date with her and Danny? That hadn't been part of the plan, had it?

"I just thought...I mean, I'll totally blow it if it's just the two of us." Elda held up her phone. "I can't even handle texting."

Holly rubbed her left temple. Elda was dead right. She'd tried texting Danny last night after the gingerbread kick-off thing, and it had been a near catastrophe. Holly had been down in the kitchen helping her mom pack up Grandma's china, and she'd left Elda alone upstairs with her phone. Danny had texted her: "What's your recipe for royal icing?" and Elda had totally flubbed it, sending Danny a dictionary-sized pile of babble—going from her favorite kind of frosting to the time her brother Sal had tried to hide the evidence that he'd eaten part of their dad's birthday cake by shoving it down the garbage disposal, fork and all, and Elda had to take the whole sink apart. She'd even managed to sneak something in there about Sal's issues with clogging up the plumbing. The whole conversation was a disaster. It was like The Coffee Shop Incident on steroids.

Holly had to perform triage. She took the phone from Elda and wrote, "OMG! Sorry. My little cousin got a hold of my phone and was being a jerk." Holly shot Elda an accusing eye.

"You had me wondering..." Danny wrote back.

"So embarrassing! And shame on you for trying to steal my royal icing recipe!" She sent him a gif of Veronica Mars wagging a finger. Then he sent her a gif of some basketball player doing it, too, and then the whole thing devolved into a thirty-minute gif off.

The time flew by. Holly'd planned on ending the conversation right away, just kind of shooting him a quick "good night" or something, but then he sent her a gif of a little girl crying while her gingerbread house crumbled with the caption "you," and Holly couldn't back down from that challenge. She summoned everything she ever knew about Danny Garland, remembering that he was a big LEGO dork as a kid, so she sent him the same caption attached to a gif from *The LEGO Movie* of a guy running around with no pants.

Holly was texting Danny Garland. Yeah, he thought he was talking to Elda, but she, *Holly*, was talking to him, as herself, really. Her stomach fluttered every time the phone buzzed with a new message. Holly lost track of time and space. She tuned out the sounds of her extended family playing cards downstairs. She forgot that Elda was in the room with her. All that mattered in the world was impressing Danny with her gif recall.

Holly ended the conversation by pulling out the big guns—Madeline Kahn from *Clue* saying, "Flames on the side of my face"—and handed the phone back to Elda, who had fallen asleep on the pull out couch during Holly and Danny's text exchange. "You do not even think about texting him without consulting me first," Holly'd said. "Got it?"

Elda had nodded. "You're the boss."

Correct. Holly was the boss.

"I think you're right, though, about needing a buffer." Holly checked out the other people walking up and down Main Street this morning. She guessed most of them were on candy-finding missions. "Maybe I should come with, at least on the first date. But I'm not going out with that Brian guy. We have to find somebody less objectively awful." She was willing to do practically anything for her cousin, but dating Danny Garland's brother was a bridge too far.

"I will help you find that guy," Elda said. "I'll be your wingwoman. I'm way better at talking to guys when I'm not pursuing them myself. I promise."

"Fabulous."

Holly pulled open the door to the candy shop, into which about half the population of North Pole had crammed itself. Yelling and screaming muffled the Bing Crosby Christmas soundtrack pumping through speakers on the walls. It was like the candy version of one of those wedding dress clearance sales on sitcoms. A girl with long, curly, blond hair had about sixteen packages of M&Ms in her arms, and she protected them like a running back, Heisman pose and all. Some guy was stuffing bags of gummy bears into a garbage bag. "Wow," Holly said, as a box of Twinkies sailed past her face. Then she snapped into gear and tossed her coffee in the garbage. It would only slow her down. "Grab whatever you can." She saluted Elda. "I'll see you on the other side. Good luck!"

Holly dashed down the nearest aisle and started pulling stuff off the shelves, without stopping to think—she got the licorice she needed plus Skittles and Fun Dip and every color of Sixlet available. She hadn't thought to bring a bag, so she pulled off her sweater to use as a sack.

She dodged a couple arguing about gimmicky Oreo flavors as she took a hard right into the next aisle. There she saw them. The Take 5 bars. They transported her back to the gingerbread contests from when she was a kid. Danny Garland had loved Take 5 bars. He'd said once, after receiving his blue ribbon, that he never used them in his showstoppers, but he'd always buy a few to eat. A full box of them sat on the shelf a few feet away.

She dove for them just as some guy—a dude in his twenties with acid-washed mom jeans that may or may not have been worn ironically, Holly couldn't tell—lunged for the same box. Holly threw her body between the guy and the candy and grabbed the Take 5 bars.

"Off-sides!" he yelled, rolling away from her on the floor. "You can't bogart all the supplies."

"You snooze, you lose." Holly tucked the box of Take 5 bars safely into her sweater.

A red flush of anger crept up his cheeks. "You're going down, you know that?"

"Craig."

Both Holly and the guy spun toward the end of the aisle. Another dude, about the same age as Craig but wearing a uniform from the arcade, stood there, hands on hips, one dark eyebrow raised. He looked like a superhero. A nerdy superhero, but a superhero nonetheless.

"She stole all the Take 5s, Dinesh," Craig whined.

"She stole nothing. This is a store. Those bars don't belong to you. Besides, I have some candy at home you can use." Holly didn't know who this Dinesh guy was, but thank goodness he showed up. Elda appeared behind Dinesh at the end of the aisle.

"Is everything all right?" she asked.

Dinesh nodded. "Everything's fine. Just keeping the

peace."

Craig and Dinesh left, and Elda came running over to Holly. "You okay?"

"I'm fine." Holly triumphantly held up the box of Take 5 bars. "I've got your ticket to Danny Garland success right here."

The girls paid for their stuff, then they stopped at the grocery store and the bakery. By the time they'd gotten through all of Main Street, they had at least twenty pounds of candy. The girls brought it all back to Grandma's garage, which they were going to use as a workshop. It was the most secluded place available, since the actual house was teeming with people and littered with boxes and garbage bags of Grandma's old stuff.

While Elda swept the floor, trying to clean up the garage as best she could, Holly retrieved the Take 5 bars and arranged them on a sheet, which she'd draped over a few chairs like a photography studio backdrop. The dark brown wrappers popped against the stark, white fabric. She stood back and admired her work. Holly could arrange a kickass still life. She motioned to Elda. "Give me your phone."

Elda handed it over, and Holly took the photo, which she sent to Danny. "I know these used to be your favorites." She added a candy bar emoji for good measure.

As they waited for him to respond, Holly and Elda took inventory of their candy, spreading an old bed sheet over a banquet table. While Elda stared at her phone, Holly walked around the perimeter of the table, turning bags of Skittles and M&Ms over and around in her hands, feeling the pieces whoosh from one end of the bag to the other. She stood multi-flavored candy canes on end in a World's Best Grandma mug. Then she separated the gumdrops by color into bowls—red, green, orange, yellow, purple, and white—popping a few into her mouth here and there for quality control. Once she had everything unbagged and organized the way she liked and had written a threatening note to her cousins and brother to stay away from their stash "OR ELSE," she sat on a folding chair in front of the display with her raggedy old sketch pad and a pencil.

Holly drew in a deep, calming breath. Now was the time to brainstorm. She touched the tip of her pencil to the paper.

"Oh my God! He wrote back." Elda tossed Holly the phone like it was a bomb.

Holly dropped her pencil and caught the phone. The moment for inspiration had vanished. She looked down at what Danny had written. "You remembered that?" the message said.

"Oh my God. Oh my God." Elda paced the garage floor, as she unwrapped one of the rainbow-colored lollipops from the bakery.

"We need that, Elda," Holly said.

Elda shoved the lollipop right into her mouth.

Rolling her eyes, Holly turned her attention back to the phone. What to say to Danny? Did he think it was weird or cool that she remembered his candy preferences? Holly decided to play coy. "Of course I remembered. I have a dossier on every single North Pole gingerbread competitor. I'm very thorough."

"Oh, really," Danny said. "What else do you know about people?"

"I know Craig handles disappointment poorly and that his friend Dinesh has to calm him down."

"Well, everyone knows that." Danny kept typing, and Holly had to stop herself from grabbing her own piece of candy to distract her while waiting. Finally, his message popped up. "I think it's sweet that you remembered. Get it? Sweet? Candy? I was trying to make myself look like less of a dweeb by pointing out that pun, but I think it backfired."

Grinning, Holly wrote him back. "It definitely backfired. And you may think it's 'sweet' that I remembered, but I'm only trying to lull you into a false sense of security. I want you to trust me. Then I'll pounce." And a cat emoji.

"Consider me lulled," he said. "What are you doing now?"

Holly's heart slammed against her chest. Her second text conversation with Danny Garland was no less exciting than the first. "Hanging out in the garage," she said. "Want to come over?" Oh my God, she'd just asked him over. Who was she?

"I'll be there as fast as my crutches can carry me." He punctuated that with a winky face.

Holly tossed the phone back to Elda. "There you go. He's on his way here." Holly had reeled him in, and now it was time to let her cousin do some of the work.

Elda stared at the phone. "He's...coming here?"

"Yeah. He wants to see the girl who remembered his favorite candy bar." Danny was probably grinning big right now, loping over here on his crutches. For Elda. Not for Holly. It was important to keep remembering that.

"What do I say to him?" Elda asked.

"Talk about our day. Tell him about all the battles we fought in town."

Elda grabbed another lollipop, but Holly batted it out of her hand. They needed every ounce of that candy. "It's too much pressure." Elda started pacing. "All I can think about are those scorpion suckers we found at the gift shop and the chocolate-covered crickets."

"Do *not* talk about the crickets." Holly placed her hands on her cousin's shoulders and looked her straight in the eye. "You can do this. Tell him we went to Santabucks, and that we missed seeing him there. Say he's way better at making coffee than his brother." All day Holly had been watching for

Danny out of the corner of her eye, practicing what she'd say to him if and when she saw him, assuming she was someone who looked like Elda and had the confidence that went with all that genetic good fortune. "Tell him you were hoping to see him around town, that you imagined running into him in the M&M aisle at the candy shop, that you were distracted all day because, as much as you want to win this competition, you realized somewhere around the Lemondrops that you wanted to see him more."

"Wow..." Elda's eyes got all dreamy and glassy. "That's way better than the bug thing."

"He'll love it coming from you," Holly told her. "Believe me."

Chapter Six

Danny's judgment with girls was totally faulty. Today just proved it.

Elda was hilarious. She was smart and sweet, and she remembered that his favorite candy bar was a Take 5. He'd gone all gaga for Holly in person, but Elda…she *got* him. She understood him. That was way more important than some stupid tattoo. Anyone could get one of those.

He grabbed his crutches and booked it next door to Mrs. Page's garage. He'd ask Elda to hang out. The bakery was sponsoring an event tonight—the Sugarplum Sweets competition. Some of his friends from school were competing in it, and he promised he'd watch. Besides, it'd be a low-pressure first date—not much talking required.

When he opened the side door of the garage, he found Holly and Elda sitting on chairs flanking a table, staring at a mound of sweets that covered an entire king-size sheet. Holly slammed a sketch pad shut and shoved it under her seat when Danny walked in.

His heart skipped a beat when he saw Holly with a pencil

stuck behind her ear. He knew it couldn't be the case, but it almost felt like she was mirroring him. Ever since the accident, he always had a pencil over his ear. Maybe she'd noticed.

Oh, who was he kidding? No, she hadn't. It wasn't like he was the first person to ever put a pencil behind his ear.

Danny gripped the handles on his crutches, focusing on Elda. Elda was the one who liked him. Elda was the one who'd sent him gif after gif of people wagging their fingers. Elda was the one who knew he loved Take 5 bars. And she was very, very pretty. Like, no one would debate him on that.

"So here's where all the candy went." He'd just returned from driving around town with Jamison, hunting for ingredients to make his gingerbread showstopper. North Pole had been cleaned out. The only stuff left at the sweet shop had been brown Sixlets and discounted items from Halloween and Thanksgiving—like white chocolate turkeys and those gross peanut butter things in the orange and black wax wrappers.

Elda jumped up and fetched him a chair, which was super nice. "We'd be happy to share some of our candy with you."

"Elda," Holly said, eyeing the candy stash, "stop giving away our stuff." She nodded to Danny. "Though you can have the Take 5 bars, obviously."

"It's all right." Danny sat down and put his leg up. The garage was musty and smelled of mildew, but at least it wasn't too cold. "I don't need your charity. What are you guys building?"

"It's gonna be amazing!" Elda said. "We're build—"

Holly stomped on her cousin's foot, keeping her from spilling the beans. "Nice try. Like we'd tell you."

"So, um, Danny." Elda faced him, sitting on the edge of her seat. Her hands were folded in her lap, and she stared at him with big, brown doe eyes. "I was hoping to run into you in town today."

"Yeah?"

"I just...I kept peeking around every corner, waiting for you to pop out"—her hands turned into claws, like she'd been imagining Danny as a bear or something—"and surprise me. Grrr!"

Holly kicked Elda in the shin.

"Ow!" Elda rubbed her leg. "I mean, our texting...wow. And I found the Take 5 bars, so." She shrugged.

Holly buried her face in her hands.

"Um, so..." Danny said. It was time to do it, even if only to put an end to the abomination of a conversation the two of them had going right now. He was going to ask out Elda Page. He hadn't asked a girl out in six years, basically. His mouth went dry. "There's this thing tonight." His voice definitely squeaked. Wow, he was pathetic at this.

"Holly!" a boy's voice boomed from outside. "Where are you?"

Danny's throat clamped up. Who was this dude yelling for Holly? Maybe she had a boyfriend. It was entirely possible. Maybe that, and not some other reason, was why Holly was so completely uninterested in him.

"Garage," she shouted.

A guy about Danny's age walked in, and, wow, this dude was competition. He was tall and muscular with dark, wavy hair and chiseled features. And he was looking for Holly. No wonder she didn't like Danny.

The guy's eyes went right to Elda. "Oh, there you are. You're the one I'm looking for, actually." He rubbed his bare arms. "What the hell are you two doing out here? It's freezing."

"Try putting on a coat, Sal. It's Minnesota," Holly said.

Elda gestured toward the guy. "Sal, Danny. Danny, Sal. My little brother."

"Oh, hey." So, he was Holly's cousin. Danny's stomach dropped even harder than before. Since Sal wasn't Holly's boyfriend, she was definitely rejecting Danny for reasons that had everything to do with Danny himself.

Sal grinned sheepishly at his sister as he ran his fingers through his hair. "I was looking for you, because I need some help...?"

Elda's shoulders dropped. "Dude."

A snicker escaped from Holly's lips, but she covered her mouth and kept her eyes on the mountain of candy. It was the first time Danny had heard her laugh. It was cute, musical, more girly than Danny would've expected.

Sal winced. "Sorry."

"You're seventeen," Elda said. "You're fully capable of handling this yourself."

Danny's glance bounced between Elda and Sal. They had their sibling shorthand down pat.

"Obviously, I'm not," Sal said.

"Well, you need to learn." Elda raised her eyebrows.

"So, teach me." Sal pointed to the door. "No time like the present."

Groaning, Elda hoisted herself from the floor and said, "Be right back."

Once they'd left the garage and were back in the house, Holly let out the giggle she'd been holding in. The whole garage filled with the tinkling sound of her laughter.

Danny eyed her warily, trying hard not to grin himself, which was hard. Her laugh was infectious. "What? What's she doing for him?"

Holly clamped a hand over her mouth, and her skin went pink to her hairline. "God, ugh. I shouldn't be laughing. It's not funny." She took a deep breath to calm herself. "There. Okay. Never mind."

"What?"

She pressed her lips shut again, and her eyes started watering. But despite all her effort, another laugh escaped her lips. "Damn it." She chuckled again, which made Danny start laughing. He couldn't keep it in anymore.

"I don't even know what we're laughing about," he said.

"And I'm not going to tell you." She stood and shook her arms out, centering herself. "It's gross."

"Well, now you have to tell me. My mind has gone to some very dark places."

Holly covered her mouth, and a wayward snort escaped her. "It's not funny. I laugh when I'm uncomfortable." She leaned down and grabbed a handful of orange gumdrops. She handed a few to Danny, her soft fingertips touching his palm. Danny's whole body shivered.

"It's the plumbing here," Holly said, putting a few feet of space between them. "It can't handle Sal's..." She held out her hands and shrugged. Her face went pink again.

Danny felt his own face flush. "Ah. Some little cousin got a hold of Elda's phone last night and mentioned something about this. I thought it was a joke."

"No, not a joke. Like, forever this has been a thing." Holly's breath made clouds in the chilly air. "Sal's too embarrassed to ask anyone but Elda for help. She's the toilet whisperer."

So, the girl he'd come here to ask out was known to her family as "The Toilet Whisperer." Okay. "Well, if you're going to have a superpower..."

Holly nodded in agreement. "I mean, the fact that she has one at all is impressive."

This bathroom conversation could be over, as far as Danny was concerned. "Do you have a superpower?"

Holly popped another gumdrop in her mouth and chewed thoughtfully. "Invisibility."

Danny winced playfully and straightened up taller to

whisper. "I hate to break it to you, but I think your power has worn off. I mean, I can see you."

She squinted. She was wearing lime green eye shadow behind her thick, red plastic glasses. "But do you? Do you really? Or is your mind just playing tricks on you?"

"Wow. Now I'm starting to think your actual superpower is playing mind games."

The two of them glanced out the garage door to the house. No Elda.

"Does this usually take a while?" Danny asked.

"Depends." Holly bit her upper lip for a moment. "Elda's awesome. I mean, who do you know who can fix a clog, while being so discreet about it?"

"No one," he said. "Absolutely no one. And she remembered I like Take 5 bars."

Holly flushed. "Yeah, see? Awesome."

Danny checked his phone. The Sugarplum Sweethearts competition started soon. "Can I ask you something?"

"Shoot."

"Elda. Is she just this nice to everyone, or does she actually like me?"

Holly looked him right in the eye. The lights above glinted off her chartreuse eye shadow. "She likes you. Honest." She bit her upper lip again. "She remembered your favorite candy bar for eight years. I'd say she's liked you for a while."

Danny glanced at the door again. He used to sit by his front window around Christmastime and wait to see if Mrs. Page's granddaughters were coming to visit each year, ever since his family moved into their house next door. Now they were here, and one of them had remembered his favorite candy bar since they were ten.

He was going to ask Elda to hang out. That was how these things went. Girl likes boy, boy likes girl, boy asks girl out. Right?

Danny's mouth went dry again. He hadn't done this kind of thing for a while—not since the early days of his relationship with Star. That was his main problem. He was nervous. He was scared of rejection, so his body was reacting negatively to asking Elda out.

He glanced at Holly, who'd sat down again and was looking over her candy supply. Her back was to Danny, and he couldn't help but notice the smooth slope of her neck, and her short, soft hair. He wanted to run his fingers through it, against the grain. He wanted to kiss up, up, up her neck to the rounded spot right behind her ear. He wanted...the wrong girl.

Danny picked up his crutches and stood from his chair. He had to get out of here. "Hey, tell Elda I had to go. I'll text her later, okay?"

Holly raised a hand in a silent good-bye. She didn't turn around as Danny left the garage.

• • •

Tuesday, December 19

"On your marks," the mayor said. "Get set... Decorate!"

Holly grabbed a gingerbread figure from the ornate Christmas-themed platter in front of her. "You ready for this?" she whispered to Elda.

Hands shaking, Elda picked up her own cookie and placed it carefully in front of her, like it was a baby bird she was trying not to smoosh. "I think so."

"Just follow my lead. We've got this."

The first round of the gingerbread competition—cookie decorating—was taking place at the fancy French restaurant in town, Joyeaux Noel. All the contestants had their own round tables, spread throughout the dining room. Last night, Holly had sent a silent prayer to Grandma that her team's table would be situated far away from Danny Garland's, but no such luck. He was right next to her and Elda.

Holly's task for the next hour was to make Danny believe she was a bumbling fool and Elda was the master decorator, all while trying to win the dang thing. Tall order.

Holly snuck a peek at Danny. He was working from a chair with his leg elevated and was loading his piping bag with royal icing. He shot the girls a smile—a gorgeous, happy smile—and a thumbs-up. Holly nudged Elda to smile back at him as Holly pursed her lips and stared at her cookie. Her joints had turned to jelly.

She picked up her own piping bag and started dictating the assignment in her mind, trying to force out all thoughts of Danny Garland. First, she snipped off the corner of a plastic bag. Then she stuck a decorating tip through the hole and filled the bag with icing. Each person had to decorate twelve gingerbread humans in a half hour—yes, teams of two had to complete twenty-four cookies.

She handed the bag she'd prepared to Elda, who'd never done it before. Without a second thought, Elda started piping icing onto the cookie in a jagged pattern. Parts of her line were way too thick; parts were too thin. In some spots, the line had been broken. This wasn't going to work. If Holly left the decorating to Elda, they'd be in last place when all was said and done.

Holly reached past her cousin and pulled Elda's pitiful cookie toward her. "Damn it!" she said out loud, slapping herself on the forehead.

Danny glanced over at Holly's outburst, and she held up Elda's tragically decorated gingerbread person. "I'm hopeless." She slumped her shoulders and pouted.

"At least you've got Elda on your team," he said.

Holly patted Elda's shoulder. "Thank goodness."

She bent over the cookie and started wiping off Elda's

piping work while Elda started another cookie.

"Thank you." Elda hovered close, talking through her teeth like a ventriloquist. She gave Holly's wrist a quick squeeze.

"No problem." Holly patted Elda's hand. "Like Danny said, we're a team. You do what you can. I'll work as fast as humanly possible." Holly was going to have to decorate all twenty-four. There was no way around it.

She craned her neck to see Danny's work. His piping was perfect, and he was already on cookie number two. This was the kid she remembered. This guy was precision personified. Despite the sinking feeling in her gut that she and Elda were going to completely bomb the first round, she couldn't help smiling. Maybe he was a total fox now, but he was still a gingerbread dork at heart.

Holly and Elda tacitly worked out a system. Elda would slowly, methodically work on one cookie, doing her absolute best, and Holly'd rush through the rest of them. It was their only hope.

"Hey," Danny whispered from the table next to them.

"We're working," Holly said. She clumsily shot a clump of frosting onto Elda's sleeve for good measure while he was watching, then she grabbed a wet towel to wipe it off.

"I know. I wanted to say I watched that documentary you told me about last night." Danny smiled at Elda.

Holly's stomach dropped to her knees. Shoot. The documentary.

After Danny had left yesterday and Elda had returned to the garage, the girls talked about the whole Danny situation. He'd just sent Elda another message restating how much he loved the candy bars. "You need to keep helping me with him," Elda had said. "If it hadn't been for you, I never would've known about the Take 5 bars. Now he thinks I'm, like, this incredibly thoughtful girl."

"Well, you are," Holly said. "And you'd totally have bought him those candy bars on your own if you'd known they were his favorites."

Elda narrowed her eyes. "Yeah, probably."

"Definitely."

"I think he actually likes me." All the blood had drained from Elda's face.

"Which is the point of all this." Holly'd pulled out her sketch pad and started working. She had a showstopper to build.

"Right," Elda had said. "But Danny likes me because of something you did. What if we go out and he's totally bored with me?"

"You could never be boring," Holly'd said. "Give yourself a little credit. But if you want me to keep chatting him up for you, I will." Holly loved the rush of seeing how grateful Danny had been for the kindness. He deserved someone good and sweet and awesome, someone like Elda. Holly was more than happy to choke down her own feelings for that.

So she and Elda had hopped on the phone with Danny again last night. The girls had made an evening of it—eating popcorn on their pull out couch in the attic, while Holly's thumbs did the talking and Elda brushed makeup all over Holly's face. Danny and the girls texted back and forth about all kinds of things—from North Pole gossip to how they were never going to watch *Game of Thrones* because it was too popular.

Elda had screwed the cap back on her mascara and passed Holly a hand mirror. "But I like *Game of Thrones*!"

"No, you don't." Holly grimaced at her reflection. Elda hadn't done beauty makeup, like Holly had assumed. Her face was covered in bruises and scars. "Not liking *Game of Thrones* is better, more interesting."

Elda shrugged. "You know best." That was when Elda

had traipsed downstairs to play hide-and-seek with Aunt Vixi's kids.

Danny filled Holly in on everything from who was hooking up with whom in town to the drama between her grandma and the town's baker, Nancy—both of them liked Frank from the hardware store. Frank was a player! Holly had told Danny to check out a Netflix documentary about the Mitford sisters from the book she was reading.

And she'd forgotten to tell Elda to study up on the rest of their conversation.

"Totally fascinating." Danny was on his sixth gingerbread person by now. "You were right. I did some digging on the Mitford sisters last night. Who do you think was the worst one?"

Elda would not have an answer for this question. She knew nothing about the Mitfords.

Holly broke off the head of her current gingerbread figure on purpose, to create a diversion. "Oh, no!" she cried.

"What happened?" Danny craned his neck to see their station.

"One of our cookies broke." Elda held up the headless cookie to show Danny. She patted Holly on the shoulder. "It's okay. We'll get a new one." She turned back to Danny. "And obviously Diana was the worst sister."

Good save, Elda. Though she should've spoken up before Holly went and destroyed one of their cookies.

Elda, still taking charge, raised her hand and caught the attention of the mayor. "One of our cookies broke." She put on a pouty face that had probably gotten her out of many a traffic ticket.

The mayor shook his head. "Sorry, ladies. Twelve cookies each. That's all you get. Make sure the ones you have left are perfect."

"Shit," Holly said. She never would've sabotaged a cookie

if she had known.

"I'll give you one of mine."

Both girls' heads swiveled over to the table on their other side, the not-Danny side. Dinesh was there, still in his arcade uniform. He brushed an errant black curl off his forehead and handed Elda a clean cookie. "I'm going to lose anyway," he said with a wink.

"You're our hero, Dinesh," Elda said, and he waved her off, turning his attention back to his remaining eleven cookies. "That was super nice," Elda whispered to Holly. "Maybe you should go out with him. He could be the fourth in our double date."

Shrugging, Holly focused on her current cookie. Dinesh was cool. He'd come to her rescue twice in the past two days. But he'd given up one of his gingerbread figures to help his rival. He didn't care about the competition. Danny hadn't offered the girls one of his cookies—he'd probably never even considered giving them one of his cookies—because he knew what it took to win, and he understood that all was fair in love and gingerbread. Holly respected his competitive spirit. Still, "Dinesh is better than that Brian guy for sure. Set it up."

Elda squeezed Holly's wrist. "I'm on it."

Holly peeked over at Danny, who was piping a delicate pattern on one cookie's tummy. "Tell him you like his filigree technique."

"What?" Elda whispered.

"Just do it. He'll eat it up."

Elda skirted around Holly so she was on Danny's side again. "Your filigree technique is really something."

Grinning, Danny held up the cookie he was currently working on. "You think?"

Elda nodded. "Super good. Very nice." Holly was fairly certain Elda had no idea what she was talking about. Actually, "fairly certain" was an understatement.

"Thanks." Danny's whole face lit up as his eyes met Elda's. Holly had to look away as the two of them exchanged goo-goo eyes. She turned toward Dinesh instead, whom she caught also staring at Elda, because of course he was. Groaning, Holly pulled yet another gingerbread figure toward her and started piping.

This was what she'd signed up for. She repeated it in her head like a mantra.

Chapter Seven

DANNY: *OMG Craig's cookies.*

ELDA: *I didn't see. What? Were they good?*

DANNY: *They were the Starks.*

ELDA: *(gif of Jon Snow frowning amidst a blizzard)*

ELDA: *Of course he'd do Game of Thrones cookies.*

DANNY: *(gif of priestess ringing the "Shame" bell)*

ELDA: *For two people who hate Game of Thrones, we sure have a lot of gifs at the ready.*

DANNY: *Something to think about. Ask not for whom the SHAME bell tolls, it tolls for we!*

ELDA: *(crying laughing emoji X 10)*

Chapter Eight

At the end of the first round, the mayor and two other judges took their time surveying each team's gingerbread cookie entries. Danny's heart was in his throat as the three jury members swanned around the Joyeaux Noel dining room. He'd done well; he was positive of that. Danny had been worried about his rusty piping skills, but today's competition was like riding a bike. His filigree technique was on point, and Elda had noticed.

The room was full of talented decorators, like Tinka Foster. She was Nancy Gold's assistant at the bakery, and sweet stuff was her whole life. Her piping was perfectly straight and uniform, as if every decorative line had been produced by a machine. Craig wasn't the most talented piper, necessarily; but what he lacked in raw skill, he made up for in creativity.

And then there were the Page girls. Elda possessed the perfect mix of talent and artistry. Each cookie she decorated had a unique little flourish, like different hairstyles or argyle sweaters. Not only that, she had to decorate all twenty-four cookies herself, because Holly was not up to the task, what with breaking the head off of one cookie and glopping on her frosting with the finesse of an elephant on roller skates.

But Holly had impressed Danny, too, in a way. He couldn't see her work from where he was sitting during the competition, but he could tell she'd been pushing hard, trying her best not to let Elda down. That took guts to stand next to her more talented cousin and try her best, even though her best was, honestly, pretty terrible.

He glanced over at Elda, who was still standing behind their table, talking to Dinesh, while Holly had flitted off somewhere.

Elda was definitely gorgeous. She was, as Brian was quick to point out, one of the most beautiful girls who'd ever stepped foot in North Pole. And she liked him. She was smart and well-read. She liked history and architecture.

Elda was obviously the perfect girl for him. If someone were to ask Danny to make a list of the most important traits he'd want in a girlfriend, they'd all add up to Elda. The two of them just needed the chance to spend some time alone, without the distraction of Holly.

The room buzzed with life as the other contestants, their friends and families, and the gaggle of tourists who lined the walls chatted and laughed while the judges made their way around the room. When the trio of judges stopped at Danny's table to evaluate his work, he held his breath, scared to look at them. Giving nothing away, the mayor and his judge buddies whispered "Mmm-hmms" and "Uh-huhs" as they lifted up each cookie and examined Danny's piping. A few moments later, they'd moved on to Elda's table, and Danny finally exhaled.

Elda, totally poised and cheerful, smiled at the judges as they came over. She shook their hands and greeted them with a warm hello. From his spot against the wall, Elda's brother

Sal clapped like a trained seal. "Team Page!" he shouted. Elda chuckled.

Danny had to do something nice for her, to thank her for the Take 5 bars.

The perfect idea came to him like a million little Christmas lights blinking on; even though the judging for this round wasn't over yet, Danny considered bolting straight out of the restaurant and running home as fast as his crutches could carry him.

About a year ago, Elda's grandmother had given Danny an old, tattered book on architecture, specifically famous Midwestern buildings, since she knew Danny had an interest in the subject. She'd told him then that one of her granddaughters was also well-versed in the subject, which was probably why she'd been so good at the gingerbread contest.

Danny still had the book, along with some other magazines she'd given him over the years. He'd return them to Elda today, accompanied by a romantic invite—he'd buy tickets for the North Pole architecture tour. It'd be the perfect first date.

He glanced over at Elda again. The judges had left her table by now, and she was back to chatting with Dinesh. The two of them were laughing about something. A sour feeling settled in Danny's stomach. Anxiety, that's all this was. Giddy nerves and excitement manifesting themselves as sickness. He was about to ask out his dream girl. It was a very good thing, no matter what his gut was trying to tell him.

The mayor and the other judges went to the middle of the floor, and everyone around the room stood up straighter as the mayor started speaking. "We saw so many delicious looking gingerbread people on these tables today. The spirit of Christmas, as always, is alive and well in North Pole." The mayor's eyes twinkled as he surveyed the room. "But enough sappiness. Let's get to the scores." He glanced down at the paper in his hands. "In third place so far, Ms. Tinka Foster."

Tinka jumped up and down, squealing, as Sam tried to wrap her in a hug. Tinka was off to a good start. Their scores in this round carried over into the second and third.

Danny's palms were sweating. He'd never lost this round before. Never ever. Ever.

"In second place," the mayor said, "Elda and Holly Page. Your grandma would be proud."

Elda high-fived Dinesh at the table next to her, and Danny's eyes swooped around the room, instinctively hunting for Holly. She was standing over by the punch bowl, ladling herself a cup of eggnog. She glanced up as if she felt Danny's eyes on her. She didn't smile. In fact, she scowled and looked away.

The sickening dread in his stomach was gone, replaced by tingly excitement and disappointment. He hated that she looked at him with such distaste, like she didn't think he was good enough for Elda or something, like she saw right through him and was completely disenchanted. He desperately wanted to change her mind.

Mayor Sandoval continued, "In first place is...ho, ho, ho! Danny Garland, the comeback kid!"

The crowd cheered loudly for him as Danny accepted a certificate of achievement from the mayor. This gingerbread contest was supposed to be the thing that fixed all his problems, but all he felt was numb.

• • •

Holly rubbed her temples. "Okay. Maybe we should put this on hold and practice the gingerbread houses instead." She plucked her pencil and sketch pad out of Elda's hands and tossed them aside. Elda really, really, really wanted to help Holly with their sketches for the showstopper, but—and it pained Holly to even think this—Elda sucked at gingerbread. Not only had she been awful while piping the frosting earlier today during round one, but she didn't appear to have an artistic bone in her body. She kept trying to add different ornaments to the sketches that'd completely throw off the balance of the entire showstopper.

Elda popped yet another gumdrop into her mouth, even though Holly had asked her repeatedly to stop eating all their candy. They'd already lost three bags of Skittles to Aunt Vixi's kids, who had not been deterred by Holly's threatening note. "This gingerbread thing is hard work, huh?"

Yes, yes, it was, but that was news to Elda. Holly'd started building gingerbread houses when she was in preschool, and she kept making them even after her family stopped coming to North Pole for Christmas. Getting a bunch of cookies to stand upright while loaded down with candy and frosting took skill and practice.

But Holly had to stop holding the fact that Elda was a novice against her. Elda had always been the one to keep the team fed and hydrated. She may not have helped on the actual showstopper, but she provided a valuable service. She was and always had been, as far as Holly was concerned, an integral part of the team. Holly had to keep reminding herself of that.

"We'll worry about the showstopper later. For now we need to concentrate on round two." Holly opened up one of the gingerbread house kits Elda had found at a grocery store, complete with some bastardization of royal icing. Holly grabbed scissors and opened it anyway. "If you can learn to make a gingerbread house stand using this garbage, you'll have no trouble making one stand tomorrow during the competition using the real stuff."

The girls stood at their worktable, trying to erect a house on a tiny bit of cardboard using store-bought gingerbread and icing. Holly showed Elda how to make a base of royal icing to help the walls hold, and how to line them up at perfect angles. "Basically, our goal is twofold," Holly said, her sticky frosting-covered hands holding two walls upright as the icing dried. "Make sure the thing stays standing, and make it look pretty. Both elements count for a lot. As long as it stays up, we won't get docked too badly for, like, frosting seeping out the cracks or whatever. And if we can decorate it nicely, that goes a long way, too."

Elda spread more frosting along the crack between the two walls. "Thank you for helping me."

"Of course," Holly said.

"I mean, with this, but also with Danny. I think it's working." Elda furrowed her brow as she held the walls together in some approximation of a right angle. "Danny said he's going to stop by soon."

"Ooh." Holly tried hard to feign excitement. She'd known the score going in—Holly would do the work, but Elda would reap the benefits. And the benefits were considerable. Danny Garland was a beautiful, sweet, smart boy, and Holly's crush on him had only gotten bigger.

"I talked you up to Dinesh today," Elda said.

"Mmm-hmm." Holly never should've given Elda the okay on that. She didn't want Dinesh. She didn't want anyone here in North Pole except Danny. It wouldn't be fair to Dinesh for her to agree to go out with him when she definitely wasn't interested.

"He seemed kind of into it," Elda said.

Sure, *kind of.* And that was the other thing. Dinesh didn't like Holly; that much was obvious. He, like Danny and most other people who were attracted to girls, liked Elda. If Dinesh had in any way indicated that he'd be interested in dating Holly, it was probably only as a way to spend time with Elda. "You know what? I'm good," Holly said. "Maybe we should nix the whole double date idea. I don't need you to set me up."

"I want to," Elda said. "You're so great to help me with Danny and the gingerbread contest. Give me a chance to do the same for you. Grandma would've wanted us both to be happy."

Dinesh wasn't going to make Holly happy. "I'm honestly fine." A wave of sadness hit her, which was nothing new. All her emotions were so near the surface here in North Pole, especially since they were staying in Grandma's house and going through Grandma's things. And every day, the house got a little emptier, a little less Grandma-like. She would've wanted both girls to be happy, but that didn't seem possible, given the current situation.

The side door of the garage opened, and in came Danny, the very reason for Holly's emotional confusion.

Carrying a Christmas gift bag over his shoulder, he maneuvered his crutches past their gingerbread paraphernalia on the floor and took a seat in an empty lawn chair. Elda jumped up and got him another chair for his leg.

"Thanks." He grinned at her as he hoisted his leg up. "What are you up to?"

"Practicing." Elda stood next to Holly at the table and grabbed a bowl of icing. "Now put that wall here, Holly." She took Holly's hand and moved it exactly where she wanted it to go. "I'm teaching Holly how to make a gingerbread house."

"I was just the water girl back when we used to enter the competition with our grandma," Holly said, shifting her hands slightly to make sure the walls were at a perfect ninety-degree angle. "I used to be the gopher. I didn't do any of the gingerbread work."

Danny's eyes met Holly's, but she pulled hers away fast. If she allowed herself to linger on him for any meaningful length of time, he'd see right through her.

"You two are never going to catch me in the second round," he said.

Holly was trying so hard to keep her cool, to show him that she'd barely noticed his existence, but he looked so cute sitting on that chair, and he kept smiling at her like she was a real person or something. Maybe he was just trying to throw them off their game by being so charming. He had to know he was a beautiful human specimen who made otherwise smart and clearheaded girls lose their cool. That couldn't be a mystery to him.

Holly doubled down on her glare, just to throw him off the scent.

"Where's your showstopper?" he asked.

"Like we'd keep it out here for you to spy on." Holly fought hard against a smile and lost.

Danny beamed at her like her smile was the one gift on his Christmas list this year. God, this guy was good at making a person feel like the only girl in the room. "Good point."

Elda nodded toward Danny's chair. "I'm working on some sketches now. My book's right under you."

"Elda," Holly warned.

"Holly, it's fine. Danny already knows what he's doing for his showstopper."

"It's true," he said. "I do."

Holly was usually very shy about showing her work to people, especially in rough draft form. Whenever their school had an art show, Holly'd make sure to grab an inconspicuous spot in a dark corner near the fire extinguisher. But showing her work to Danny was different. She wanted him to see it. He'd understand what she was going for. He'd be impressed. She needed him to see it.

"Okay, fine. Whatever." She shrugged, hands still on the gingerbread walls.

Danny reached under the chair and picked the sketch

pad up. "You sure this is okay?" he asked, slowly opening the front cover.

"Totally fine," Elda said. "We trust you."

Holly's heart sped up as he opened the cover. She couldn't look. This was a huge mistake. He was going to think she was a fraud, a no-talent poseur.

"These are good. Really good."

Holly peeked over at him. He was still flipping through the book. When he finished, he looked up, eyes squarely on Elda. "I'm super impressed. And these are totally you. I mean, I see your eye for detail and the love for your grandma, the way you've stayed so faithful to the details on her actual house."

Tears stung Holly's eyes. She'd been so worried about him thinking she sucked, that she'd completely forgotten that he was going to think those drawings were Elda's, not hers. To Danny, Elda was the talented one. Holly jumped up from her seat and held up her hands, shielding her face. "Be right back," she said. "Need to wash these."

She ran into the kitchen, where her parents and aunts and uncles were sitting at the table with their real estate agent, talking about selling the house.

"Hey, honey." Her dad motioned her over, but Holly stayed where she was, right near the door, still shielding her eyes. "There are a few interested buyers. We should be able to unload this place in no time."

"Great." Holly waved and ran to the bathroom on the second floor.

Danny and Elda were doing great. Grandma's house was about to be sold. It was too much. Holly would never be able to keep smiling for the next week and a half, not with her dad talking about passing off his childhood home to some strangers like it was an old sweater he no longer had use for, and not with having to watch Elda and Danny being all cute together, bonding over Holly's words, memories, and sketches.

She did this to herself, really. She knew that. Lots of people faced rejection, got up, and tried again. Holly was the one who'd decided to avoid hurt and embarrassment at all costs. It had kept her mostly happy. It meant no sweeping romantic love, sure, but it also meant no heartbreak. That wasn't nothing.

Holly had to endure this for another ten days. She'd be fine. She'd be great.

But when she went back to the garage, Holly found Elda kneeling next to Danny's chair, gazing into his eyes. "So, I got tickets for Tuesday afternoon," he was saying.

"Tickets?" Holly choked out. She had to make her presence known. She was not going to be a spectator for Elda and Danny's first kiss.

Danny craned his neck to see Holly at the door. His cheeks were flushed.

"Tickets?" Holly said again.

"Um..." His eyes were back on Elda. "I just asked Elda to go with me on an architectural tour of North Pole."

"He found this old book of Grandma's." Elda passed it to Holly but held on to the book for a second longer than she needed to, like she was trying to get Holly to look at her. Holly refused.

The cover of the book took Holly right back to when she was six and sitting in her grandma's den. This was an old book of all the skyscrapers in the Midwest, up to, like, 1989. It had been one of Holly's favorite books on Grandma's shelves. All the dog-eared pages, those were Holly's from when she was a kid. She'd wondered what had happened to it.

She looked up. "Wow." It came out like a whisper.

Danny pointed toward the book. "Your grandma passed

that on to me, since she knew I was interested in architecture. She'd said her granddaughter, the one who did the gingerbread contest every year, loved architecture, too. That's why I gave it to Elda."

Elda would not stop staring at Holly, so she finally gave in and looked at her cousin. Elda's face was questioning, unsure. She wanted to make sure this was okay with Holly. Well, of course it was. Holly straightened her shoulders. "That's awesome. You two will have a great time together."

"Yeah?" Elda said.

Danny was wearing a nervous, excited smile, as if he'd won the lottery. Danny would ever look at Holly like that. Guys didn't get nervous around Holly.

Danny liked Elda and Elda liked him. The two of them were nice and smart and beautiful. They deserved each other. They'd be great together. "I think that's totally fantastic."

The conversation lulled. Holly folded her arms and nodded toward the door. "So…"

"Oh, yeah," Danny said, grabbing his crutches. "I'll get going."

"You don't have to," Elda said.

"Sure he does." Holly went over to the candy table and surveyed what was left—Bottle Caps and Runts and orange slices and jelly beans. She listened as the sound of Danny's crutches faded into the distance. Holly had a showstopper to build—for the win, for her grandmother, for herself and her pride. She was letting Elda have the guy, but she didn't need to give her everything.

Chapter Nine

Wednesday, December 20

Danny took a few deep breaths as he organized the gingerbread house materials on the table in front of him. The second round of the competition was due to start at Mags's Diner any minute. The place was currently closed for business, open only to those who wanted to watch people build gingerbread houses for one hundred and twenty minutes. Tables had been spread around the room with space for two teams at each one.

Holly was across from him, sharing his table. Just Holly. Elda hadn't been able to make it. Her family needed her help with some plumbing emergency in her grandma's house.

"Good luck today," he said. Holly, too, surveyed the materials in front of her. Their task for the second round was to build a traditional, four-walled gingerbread house. It seemed simple, but sometimes the simplest things were the easiest to screw up, and Holly was no gingerbread expert. "If you need any help—"

"I'll be fine," she said, cracking her knuckles. "I built, like, four of these in the garage last night."

"Okay, but still. Those kits weren't all that great—"

"I'll be fine," she said, never even looking at him once.

Danny felt like he'd been slapped. He thought he'd made some headway with Holly the past few days. She'd started looking at him less like an annoying bug she wanted to kill and more like a helpful bug she'd let live in her garden. But now he was getting the murderous vibes again, which seemed to have resumed right after he'd asked Elda out. He hadn't meant to cause any drama. Plus, he'd assumed Holly was okay with her cousin dating him. She'd put Elda's number in his phone after all.

His upcoming date with Elda was giving him hives. He grabbed his pencil from behind his ear and scratched as deep into his cast as he could. They were so good together on the phone, but in person deafening silence took over. When Holly left the two of them alone in the garage yesterday, they literally sat in silence until Danny finally handed Elda the architecture book. And it wasn't charged, sexual tension-filled silence. It was just silence.

"Shoot!" Danny nearly fell off his chair. His cast had just devoured another pencil tip. He probably had five of them in there now.

"You okay?" Holly's glasses had slipped to the tip of her nose, and she glowered over them like a stern schoolteacher. The way her brow dipped down to a vee between her thick, perfectly arched eyebrows was a thing of beauty, which was a dumb thing for him to think, because this girl obviously thought he was annoying. Why couldn't his brain transmit that information to the rest of his body?

"Fine." He held up his pointless pencil. "Broke another one."

Holly plucked a pen from her purse and handed it to him.

"Merry Christmas." The hint of a smile on her face faded almost immediately, but Danny had caught it.

Grinning, he looked at the pen she'd given him. It was from Purdue University. "Is this where you're going—?"

He was cut off as the mayor tapped on his microphone to announce the start of the second round. After Mayor Sandoval finished his spiel, he pressed play on his favorite Christmas mix, which was just hour upon hour of Mannheim Steamroller working itself into a frenzy. As if Holly's presence hadn't caused Danny enough disturbance, the music put him on edge almost immediately. He glanced at Holly. She had pushed up the sleeves on her sweater and flipped her glasses on top of her head to appraise each piece of gingerbread, checking sizes and angles.

"Maybe you're better at this than you let on," Danny said. People always talked to their tablemates during this round of the competition. They had two hours. What were they going to do? Stand there listening to Mannheim Steamroller eviscerate "Carol of the Bells" for one hundred and twenty minutes?

"Building gingerbread houses?" Holly ran a finger across the edges of one gingerbread rectangle. "Not really, no. Like I said, I practiced a bunch last night."

Danny examined his own gingerbread. Usually focus wasn't an issue for him, but today he struggled. He drew in a deep breath and counted to three, running through all the steps in his gingerbread house building plans—erect the walls, let them dry, pipe the windows and doors—

"And I...I'm a sculptor," Holly said, after a moment.

Okay, so, maybe they weren't going to sit here in silence for two hours. Danny didn't know how to respond to this tiny fissure in her aloof facade. It was the first concrete bit of information she'd told him about herself. And it was impressive, the fact that she was a sculptor. It was something different, unique. "Are you going to study art in college?" He waved the Purdue pen at her.

She shook her head, glancing up. Since her glasses were out of the picture, Danny could see that her eyes were brown, like Elda's, but with flecks of green and yellow that added depth. She'd painted her eyelids a bright orchid, which contrasted all the colors in her irises. "No," she said. "I'm too practical for that. And I want to make money. Sorry. I know that's not the sexy answer." She grinned at him, for real, like she didn't totally despise him.

"So what's the practical thing you're going to study?"

"Ar—" She clamped her mouth shut, and something resembling panic filled her eyes. But she recovered quickly, erasing all memory of that smile from her face. "Management," she said.

Danny pointed to his own cheek. A spot of icing had landed right by Holly's nose. She wiped at it but missed.

"May I?" Danny asked. The day the Page girls first came in to Santabucks, Elda'd had a spot of chocolate on her face, and it hadn't occurred to him to tell her to wipe it off, let alone offer to remove it for her. But all he wanted right now was any flimsy excuse to touch Holly.

Her brow furrowed, she nodded. She leaned down, and he flicked away the icing. Her skin was soft and smooth, and his fingers were only about a centimeter from her lip. She was so close now, he could smell her. Holly. Warm sugar and vanilla. He wanted every room, every car, every piece of clothing in his life to smell like that.

Danny pulled his hand away and leaned back. She took the hint and stood, retreating to her station. Danny was probably just hard up, desperate for any physical contact now that he was single. He smiled, trying his best to act like her being so close to him had meant nothing. He ran his hands over a piece of gingerbread, trying to kill the sensations left behind by Holly's skin, trying to smell anything other than the trail her scent had left behind. He put a gingerbread wall to his nose and inhaled. "I'm thinking about studying architecture," he said. "Or engineering."

She nodded, but her attention was back on her gingerbread house.

"It's kind of a recent decision, actually. Ever since my leg thing, I've had to start figuring out what I really want to do with my life. This seems like a good pick. I mean, I used to think about engineering, when I was a kid. I loved to build stuff." He swiped a glob of icing onto his cardboard like it was punctuation, like that was the end of their banter. She didn't want to talk, and that was fine. He'd let her off the hook.

But after a moment, Holly asked, "You don't build stuff anymore?"

He shook his head. "Not for a long time. Not since..." He trailed off. The truth was, he hadn't done that stuff since he started focusing on basketball, since he got popular, since Star. Now he no longer had any of those things, really. Maybe he was still popular, but not in the same way. "Basketball took priority," he said. "And my social life."

She snickered. "Never a problem for me." She focused hard as she steadied her third wall. "What was your plan, though? You were going to go to college and play basketball and then..."

Danny's hands shook as he held his walls up. The icing wasn't hardening fast enough for him. "I hadn't thought past college. I never had time to think. I only had time for basketball." And hanging out. And Star.

Holly was doing the same thing he was, trying to physically hold together her house as it dried, but her hands looked a lot steadier than his did. She wasn't off-balance around him, like he was around her.

"But, like, were you going to try to play professionally, or coach, or what?"

She was still watching him, but he couldn't look her in the eye. It sounded so stupid when she said it out loud. He'd had no plans. He was going to play basketball for as long as he could, whatever that meant. He'd never in a million years suspected the end could come when he was only eighteen.

"I'm not trying to make you feel bad." Holly's voice was soft. There was no hint of sarcasm, no question as to whether or not she meant what she was saying. "I'm honestly curious. My dad has always been big on the 'back-up plan,' and honestly I agree with him. Like, I can keep sculpting and whatnot on the side, but it wouldn't hurt to learn something more practical. And after all of Elda's stuff—" She clamped her mouth shut.

"What Elda stuff?"

Holly shook her head. "Nothing. Just, she got me thinking about the whole college thing and why am I going and what do I want from it. You know? I feel like we're baby birds being pushed out of the nest, and I'm trying to figure out what to do when I hit the ground." She stepped back to admire her work so far. It looked good. Very good. So good Danny needed to shut up and focus or he'd lose this round for sure.

Holly assessed the edges of her next wall. "Is it because of Elda you're thinking about engineering again?"

Why'd she have to keep bringing up Elda? "Yeah," he said.

A faint smile appeared on Holly's lips. "You guys are perfect for each other."

For some reason, his shoulders drooped like a leaky balloon. "We are," he said. "Of course we are."

• • •

Holly's nerves still tingled where Danny's fingers had grazed her cheek. Danny Garland had touched Holly's face. He'd talked to her like she was someone worth knowing. Obviously, she had to ruin the moment it by bringing up Elda, hitting the destruct button on their conversation. It had to be done—the nuclear option.

She concentrated hard on her gingerbread house after that, and when the two hours were up, she folded her arms and stood next to her creation. This was why she was here. This was the whole point of everything.

Danny had taken the hint. He'd stopped trying to talk to her, as well. Holly kept her focus on the mayor and the judges as they worked the room, assessing every gingerbread construction.

The mayor cleared his throat, clapped for attention, and waited until all eyes were on him. The townies in the room knew to quiet down right away. The tourists took a moment to settle. "Wonderful work, everyone. You've made our job very difficult. My fellow judges and I can't wait to see what you have to offer us in the way of showstoppers on Christmas Eve. Without further ado, in third place tonight...Tinka Foster."

Tinka folded her arms, scowling, while her boyfriend tried to console her. He whispered something in her ear that made her smile. Holly had to look away. Her mind had pictured Danny doing the same to her, leaning close, the tip of his nose tickling her ear. A foolish pipedream. He liked Elda. Plus, she and Danny were polar opposites—the fun, sweet, popular guy and the introverted loner. Even if Elda weren't in the picture, Danny and Holly could never happen.

"In second place..." The mayor's eyes twinkled. "Santabucks's own, Danny Garland."

Holly checked on Danny out of the corner of her eye. He was frowning, disappointed. Danny Garland didn't do second place. Holly fought the urge to lean over and whisper a joke to him—something about how it looked like Dinesh has slathered on his royal icing with a shovel, something she would've texted him if she'd had Elda's phone—but she didn't. Danny and Holly didn't have that kind of relationship. To him she was just some random relative of the girl he liked.

Turning away from Danny, she lifted her chin. The mayor hadn't yet announced first place, and Holly was definitely in the running. Though she'd been slightly distracted by Danny during the competition, Holly had done her best. The walls of her gingerbread house were straight, the decorations looked good, and her lines were clean. She crossed her fingers and sent a telepathic message to her grandmother, wherever she might be.

"In first place tonight, we have..." The mayor paused dramatically.

Holly crossed her fingers harder.

"Holly Page!" the mayor said.

Her knees went weak. She grabbed the lip of the table to stay upright as the room erupted in applause, Danny among them. He was eyeing her curiously. "Good job," he said. "I guess I should watch out for you. If you were able to get that good at building a gingerbread house in one day..."

He trailed off into awkward silence. She battled the force pushing her toward him. This was a moment where it'd be totally normal to hug, for catharsis, in solidarity. They'd spent the past two hours working next to each other. They were friends...sort of. But Holly wasn't sure she could survive a hug.

She started gathering her things, cleaning up her table, trying to look busy, and Danny did the same, all in silence. Just as she was finishing up, Craig came over. Holly never imagined she'd be so happy to see a guy who'd once tackled her over a box of candy bars.

"What's up, Craig?" she asked cheerfully.

Craig stood in front of her and Danny in his shapeless,

high-rise jeans and a geeky Christmas sweatshirt—some *Dr. Who* joke Holly only knew by osmosis. "A bunch of us are going to the arcade for pizza. It's tradition. Wanna come?"

"I don't know." She'd been planning to work on her showstopper. She really needed to get started on that, especially now that she had a shot to win.

"Usually we only invite locals." Craig folded his arms. "But we all agreed we should make an exception for you. Your grandma was one of us, and she was a great lady."

Well, that did it. Holly pressed her tongue against the back of her upper lip for a moment to stop herself from crying. "That's nice of you," she said. "Really, really nice. Thank you. I'd love to hang out tonight."

"Me, too," Danny said, even though Holly wasn't quite sure he'd actually been invited.

• • •

"Your grandma'd talk about you all the time," Sam, Tinka's boyfriend, said as he plated pizza for Holly later that night at Santa's Playground. This was one of the North Pole places Holly had been super excited to return to. Santa's Playground was like one of the clubs that Stefon on *Saturday Night Live* always used to talk about. It had everything—video games, laser tag, pizza. Tonight it even had karaoke.

When Holly and her cousins were kids, they use to beg their parents to take them here. The moms and dads would balk, but Grandma'd always cave, letting the adults have a night out on their own so she could take her grandchildren to this magical place. The kids would spend the evening shooting each other with light-up guns and winning prizes that cost way more than they were worth.

Tonight Holly wasn't here with her cousins and brother; but these North Pole people, and the way they spoke about

Holly's grandma, almost felt like extended family. Sam, in particular, was super sweet and easygoing, and he and Tinka were so happy and in love. They were constantly finding little reasons to touch each other, but it wasn't annoying coming from them. Well, other than the fact that it made Holly wonder if she'd ever have that, if she'd ever find someone to knead her shoulders after a grueling gingerbread contest or wipe pizza sauce from the corner of her mouth.

Her eyes met Danny's for a second. He was looking at her, which was something he'd been doing a lot tonight. He had to stop that. It was like he was trying so hard to be her friend, like he needed her approval or something. Well, why? Who cared what Holly thought?

She folded her arms and stared off in the distance. She'd rather people assume she didn't care than think she cared too much. Vulnerability was not in her comfort zone.

"Why aren't you up there, Craig?" Danny nodded toward the stage at the far end of the room. A DJ had started setting up his equipment, and Dinesh had gone up to speak to the guy.

Craig folded his arms. "I'm not a karaoke DJ, Daniel."

"There's a difference?" Danny was toying with Craig, Holly could tell. This was probably their usual rapport.

"Of course there's a difference."

Dinesh dropped a few binders on the table. "You're up, Craig."

Craig saluted the table before sauntering to the stage and grabbing the mic. "Let's karaoke." His voice had dropped two octaves. Craig, in his mom jeans and *Dr. Who* shirt, started rapping to "Lose Yourself."

Holly's eyes grew as big as dinner plates, and she turned to Danny, whose chin was practically on the table. "Craig is Eminem," she said.

"We all have our niches," Dinesh explained. "Mine's Elvis."

Sam, his arm around his girlfriend, said, "Tinka and I do

movie songs."

"Your grandma used to go old school—Rat Pack stuff." Dinesh was flipping through one of the binders.

"No, she didn't." Holly's grandma did not do karaoke. She and Holly were way too similar, and Holly would never, ever get up there on her own.

"She sure did," Sam said.

"I remember." Danny's brow was furrowed. He was looking right at Holly, his eyes soft. "She sang 'New York, New York.'"

"What do you know about it?" Sam said. "I seem to remember you sitting in the corner with Star last year, making fun of us."

Danny looked down, hiding his expression, but a blush crept up his neck. "Well, Star's out of the picture now, isn't she?" He pulled one of the binders closer to him. "Maybe I'll sing tonight, too."

"Christmas miracle," Sam said.

The members of Holly's little group sang in turn— Dinesh performed a perfect rendition of "Suspicious Minds," and Tinka and Sam did an enthusiastic, if off-key, version of "Elephant Love Medley" from the movie *Moulin Rouge!*

Sam pushed a binder toward Holly. "You're up."

She shook her head "no," but couldn't deny that electricity had filled the room. The crowd at Santa's Playhouse buzzed with friendly, joyful support. If she was ever going to do it, this was the perfect place to lose one's karaoke virginity. Holly thumbed through the binder, just in case inspiration struck.

The words on the page blurred when she reached the Frank Sinatra section. Holly remembered something she'd read earlier that day. "Strangers in the Night," she said out loud.

"Good choice," Craig said.

"No, 'Strangers in the Night' was written in my grandma's

day planner under the entry for round two of the gingerbread contest. I bet that's what she was going to sing." Holly forced a smile as tears burned her eyes. Her grandma really had planned on singing tonight. She'd also had no clue she wouldn't be around to do it.

She felt Danny's eyes on her, but she couldn't look at him. It'd be too much in the moment. She was mourning her grandma. That pain was enough right now. She couldn't bear the sting of unrequited love on top of it.

Dinesh picked up the book and nodded toward the DJ. "Come on."

"Where?"

"We're going to sing 'Strangers in the Night.' For your grandma."

Holly shook her head. She barely knew that song. He couldn't expect her to get up and sing it in front of all these people.

Sam jumped up. "Yeah. Let's do it. All of us. For Mrs. Page." Sam turned to Danny. "You in?"

"You go ahead." His leg was up on a chair. "I'll be your audience. I need to save my voice for my solo."

"Fair enough." Dinesh, who had some pull at Santa's Playhouse, persuaded the DJ to let them jump the line. Holly fought against every nerve in her body telling her to run home and hide. This was for Grandma, to honor her. This was what the day planner had been instructing her to do. The five of them huddled around two microphones—Holly, Sam, Tinka, Dinesh, and Craig.

Laughing through the tears flooding her eyes, Holly let the others take the lead, keeping her distance from the mic. Arms linked, they all swayed in time to the music, belting out a slightly off-key version of the Sinatra song. She glanced over at Craig and Dinesh, who were basically treating this like an audition for *America's Got Talent*. The crowd cheered them on as they added melismatic runs to the melody.

Holly straightened her shoulders, mimicking the guys. She was always so guarded, so practiced, so calculated. She never let go like this. Even when sculpting, she kept her subject matters benign, unemotional. When dealing with matters of the heart, like with Danny, she always took the practical route. But tonight, she leaned in closer to the microphone, nudging Craig and Dinesh out of the way, and sang the final chorus as a solo.

The crowd—except Danny, because of his crutches—jumped to its feet in raucous applause. They were cheering for her. Or, well, they were cheering for the entire group, but they hadn't booed Holly after her solo. She hadn't let the team down. She hadn't let her grandma down.

Though she fought it hard, Holly couldn't stop smiling. When their group returned to the table, her eyes met Danny's accidentally. She'd kind of forgotten he was there. Almost.

After Holly sat down, Danny reached across the table and squeezed her hand, but she jerked away quickly, like she'd been burned. He wasn't supposed to touch her like that, especially not when it made her body go all weak and tingly.

"Sorry," he whispered.

"It's fine." She turned her chair so she didn't have to look at him.

The DJ called Danny's name. "I hope I'm half as good as you," he whispered, before hobbling up to the stage.

"I don't normally do this kind of thing," Danny said, once he'd situated himself behind the microphone stand, leaning forward on his crutches, "but I'm feeling inspired tonight." He got all serious then and nodded toward the DJ, who pressed play.

After the first few bars, everyone knew what song Danny was singing, and the crowd started whooping and cheering. He grinned. Danny Garland, former captain of the basketball team and person who had previously been "too cool" for karaoke, was singing Mariah Carey's "All I Want for Christmas Is You."

And he was rocking it.

His voice wasn't the best or anything, but that didn't matter. He was feeling the song. He was on crutches, yes, but he still had moves. Everyone in the crowd started singing along, cheering and clapping. Danny flipped his hair off his forehead like a total rock star, and his eyes met Holly's.

She nearly melted.

This wasn't good. Melting was not the appropriate response. All of this was getting too heady, too real. Holly rose out of her seat without really knowing what she was doing. Danny was going out with her cousin. He liked Elda. She, Holly, was the one who'd made this happen. But the way he'd just looked at her, it was almost as if he wanted her, *Holly*, which was obviously completely ridiculous.

He was being friendly. He was putting on a show. That was all this was. Holly had gone to a Justin Timberlake concert a few years ago and had wound up in the front row. She could've sworn she'd locked eyes with Justin for a moment, and maybe she had, but it had been part of the act. Danny looking at her like that just now was all part of his performance.

She had to stay cool. She was the one who was going to get hurt here.

With Danny still belting out his song, Holly ducked her head and bolted for the crowded arcade, losing herself in the lights and dings and people. She barreled to the very back of the room and hid inside the empty *Star Wars* racing game to think. She gripped the steering wheel, wishing it could transport her to outer space for real, right this second.

Holly had handed over the rights to Danny days ago. He and Elda were going on an architecture tour together in two days, their first official date. That was happening. For her own sanity, and for Elda, Holly had to stay far away from Danny. She did not want to get in the middle of this any more than she already was.

Someone knocked on the door. Holly said nothing, willing whoever it was to go away. But instead the door opened, and Danny was standing there, balancing on his crutches. Super. Just who she wanted to see. Why couldn't he just take the hint and leave her alone?

"You okay?" he said.

Holly shrugged. "I'm fine. Just playing a game." She kept staring at the welcome screen in front of her. Danny's eyes were kryptonite.

"No, you're not," he said.

"Well, I'm about to." She'd keep her sentences short and clipped. That'd give him the hint.

"You don't like me very much, do you?" he said.

Turning toward him, Holly let out a laugh, then covered her mouth, hiding her nervous chuckle. She hadn't been expecting that. Also, if only he knew.

"Did I do something?" he asked.

"Danny, oh my God."

He frowned. Man, his eyes were beautiful, especially when they were all sad like that. Sometimes she got caught up in how hot he was now, but sometimes, like in this moment, she caught a glimpse of who he was as a kid—the dorky, competitive gingerbread master, the boy who would totally understand her, if only they had the chance to get to know each other.

"Why do you care so much?" she asked. But of course he cared. Popular people always cared about being liked, because being liked was their default. That was Danny's downfall, his weakness. Holly never expected to be liked, and she found strength in that solitude. Accepting her alone status had helped her survive high school. It would help her get through the next twelve days in North Pole.

"You're always frowning at me like you think I'm an awful person, and I want to know why. What did I do to you? Was I a jerk when we were kids or something?" he asked.

Maybe she did frown sometimes. Maybe she suffered from a mild case of resting bitch face. Why did he care? He had Elda; why did he need her, too? Holly was tired and emotionally drained, and him coming around all the time wasn't helping anything. "Okay, no. I don't like you."

His jaw dropped.

Holly remembered a movie that she and her grandma used to watch back in the day—*The Journey of Natty Gann*. There was this scene where the main character had to yell at her wolf friend to send him away, because she couldn't travel with him anymore. The same kind of thing also happened in *Harry and the Hendersons*. Oh, and a few other movies she could think of. It was apparently a fairly well-worn trope.

And it was what Holly was doing to Danny right now. For her own self-preservation, she was sending him away.

"I know your type." She stood, and he had to hop away from the video game to let her out. "You're popular, but insecure. People like you can't stand it if someone doesn't adore you."

He blinked, like no one had ever dropped a truth bomb like that on him before. "You don't know anything about me."

Holly shrugged. "Maybe not."

She was nearly back to the pizza parlor when he shouted after her. "Well, you're mean and angry and you never even gave me a chance. From day one, you looked at me like you hated me."

Holly turned around and held her hands up. This had to be done. "Well, congratulations to both of us then. We don't like each other. Let's stop pretending we have anything left to discuss."

Chapter Ten

DANNY: *Okay, so, I think your cousin hates me.*

ELDA: *I guarantee she doesn't hate you.*

DANNY: *Holly said, and I quote, "I don't like you."*

ELDA: *Trust me. She doesn't hate you. She doesn't "not like" you. I know for a fact that she thinks you're nice.*

DANNY: *Too nice. She thinks I'm a puppy dog.*

ELDA: *I think she has a hard time talking to guys like you.*

DANNY: *Guys on crutches?*

ELDA: *No.*

DANNY: *Guys who used to play basketball?*

ELDA: *Don't make me say it.*

DANNY: *Well, now you have to say it.*

ELDA: *Guys with your...considerable good looks and charming personality.*

ELDA: *And now I'm blushing.*

DANNY: *So am I. Isn't it great?*

Chapter Eleven

Thursday, December 21

"I went to a bunch of your games last year," Dr. Jackson said as he paid for his coffee. "You have so much talent."

Danny opened the register and took his time gathering his doctor's change. Dr. Jackson was wearing a wool stocking cap that looked like a Santa hat, something that definitely would've been out of place anywhere else in the world. And this was the man charged with making sure Danny's leg healed okay. At least it was December. If it had been any other time of year, Danny might have found himself in the market for a new orthopedic surgeon.

"How's the leg doing, by the way?" Dr. Jackson asked. "It was such a strange injury. We don't normally see tibia breaks on the basketball court. You're a special guy, Dan."

Yay. Just another way Danny was "exceptional," though he would've preferred to be totally average in this situation, spraining an ankle or something instead of a compound shin fracture. Of course, he had to go and shatter his leg in spectacular fashion. He couldn't do anything half-assed, not even injure himself. He wondered what Holly would have to say about it. She'd probably think Danny was just trying to get attention by breaking his leg. Danny handed his customer sixty-seven cents, which the doctor promptly added to the reindeer-patterned bowl they used as a tip jar. "My leg's fine," he said.

"It's gonna heal well, Danny. You're a strong young man, and athletes do come back from these injuries. I have every reason to believe you're going to be back on the court in no time."

The last time Danny had seen the doctor, for a post-surgery checkup, he'd given Danny a timeframe of four to six months. That was no one's definition of "no time." Besides, it didn't change the fact that Danny was missing his entire senior season, or that the recruiters who'd only discovered the North Pole Reindeer because of Danny were now there to watch Kevin instead. It wasn't fair.

But at least Danny was starting to think about his future in terms other than basketball, thanks to Elda.

He handed Dr. Jackson his to-go cup and waited until he'd heard the tinkle of the bell over the door, signaling that Santabucks was finally empty, then he pulled out a notebook.

Danny was working the early morning "rush hour" today, but it was pretty slow. Christmas was only a few days away, and the people who were normally up and caffeinating themselves before work were in no hurry. At first Danny had been grateful for the slow pace—he'd planned on working out a timetable for completing his showstopper over the final days of the competition—but he was finding it hard to concentrate. His mind kept wandering back to Holly and what she'd said and whether or not she was right. The uncomfortable truth was that he still found her incredibly attractive, even though she saw him as a dumb jock who needed everyone to like him.

Well, someone did like him. Elda. And they were going on their first date tomorrow. She'd even sent him a pink heart emoji about it last night.

He got into a bit of a groove, not on his showstopper to-do list, but on a list of ways he could stop being so pathetic in front of Holly. He'd just written "Stop whining to her about how she doesn't like you," when the bell above the Santabucks door jingled, and in came Elda all by herself. Danny immediately shoved his notebook under the register and scanned the counter in front of him for something to do. Straighten napkins. That was a thing.

This was the first time the two of them had been alone together, at least since the time he asked her out. He'd been preparing himself mentally for their date tomorrow, but he had not expected to see her out in the wild this morning. This was risky and terrifying.

She gnawed on one of her long, pointy nails as she stepped up to the counter. "Hi." She kept trying to peer through the door to the back room as if looking for something, or maybe some*one*, like Jamison or Brian—some buffer to guide their conversation. Danny may have been wishing for another customer to walk through the front door himself.

"We missed you at the gingerbread contest yesterday." His voice cracked a tiny bit. Pathetic.

"Oh my God. My dad and uncle tried to change out the basement toilet by themselves, and they forgot to shut the water off, so there was this huge mess." She clamped her mouth shut for a second, then said, "It was...um...yeah."

Back at the beginning of the year, his friends Oliver and Elena had been in kind of a similar situation to what he and Elda were going through. They'd started accidentally chatting online with each other while playing this augmented reality game, but they didn't know who it was they were texting. The two of them absolutely hated each other in person. It was kind of how things were with Danny and Elda right now, minus the passionate loathing. Texting Elda was the highlight of his day. She made him think about things in a way he hadn't in a long time. For too long, he'd shut off the more intellectual side of himself, at least from the public. On the phone with Elda, he could talk about geeky things, like how he thought Corinthian columns were due for a comeback, and it was an asset, not a liability. But, in person, somehow their conversations always came back to plumbing.

"So," he said. "Did you fix it?"

She nodded. "Yeah."

And...crickets.

Danny knew what this was, at least on his end. He'd built up the impossible expectation that this was going to be some major, sweeping romance, because Elda's grandma had predicted it, because they had seemed so perfect for each other when they were kids, because their text conversations came so easily. If Danny was scared of blowing it with her in person, Elda probably was, too.

"What can I get you?" he asked.

Relief crossed Elda's face, and Danny totally got it. Coffee. Coffee was something concrete they could talk about. It was safe. "Half skim, half two percent, half caf, no foam latte with one Splenda and one Sugar in the Raw. Extra hot."

Danny started entering her order into the register.

"Oh wait, no," she said.

He looked up.

Elda was frowning. "Or should I get almond milk? I've been thinking about changing from cow's milk. What do you think?"

"Um." So, this was the kind of conversation he was doomed to have in real life with the girl he'd been texting for days about anything and everything, the girl who'd said last night that he had a "charming personality." Well, that was certainly not on display right now. Had he and Elda exhausted every topic via text, so now they were relegated to discussing milk preferences? This was not the kind of story they'd one day eagerly tell their grandchildren. "I don't know," Danny said. "Choosing the right milk. That's kind of a personal preference."

"You're right." Elda spun around as the bell above the door jingled. Danny could've sworn she'd whispered "Thank God" under her breath. He was thinking it himself.

Craig and Dinesh strolled in. Both of them looked completely drained. "Caffeine," Craig said. "We've been up all night working on our showstoppers."

"Hey, guys." Elda was positively beaming at them. She tossed her hair over one relaxed shoulder with an impressive flourish. It was not a move she'd ever used on Danny. But she was whipping her hair for Craig and Dinesh. Danny couldn't tell if she was flirting with them or if their geekiness had just made her super comfortable and unselfconscious.

"Hello, Esmerelda," Craig said.

"Did you get the toilet fixed?" Dinesh asked.

"The shower, too. Oh my God, let me show you." Elda pulled out her phone. "I have pictures. They're disgusting."

Danny had entered some alternative universe where Elda was way more excited to talk to Craig and Dinesh than she was to talk to Danny. And they seemed to have more in common, too. She and Dinesh were literally bonding over the hair and soap scum she'd pulled out of her grandma's drain. They were talking about the wads of goo in Elda's pictures with the kind of enthusiasm Danny usually reserved for basketball.

He cleared his throat. "Um, Elda. Did you decide on milk?"

She touched Dinesh's wrist. "What do you think? Combo two percent and skim or almond milk?"

Dinesh scratched his temple. "I'd go with coconut, honestly."

Elda turned to Danny. "Coconut."

Danny made her beverage as his trio of customers chatted about extreme plumbing videos on the internet. Danny mentally tossed out everything he'd learned about North Pole architecture. Those things apparently weren't going to impress Elda. He had some studying to do before his date tomorrow.

• • •

That night Holly and Elda took time out from working on their showstopper and cleaning out Grandma's house to join the North Pole natives in some Christmas merriment. People had packed St. Nicholas Park to sing carols and drink hot cocoa. Since no snow had fallen yet this month and the temperature was near fifty degrees, a game of touch football had broken out on the grass where the skating rink usually went. Kids in light jackets and no hats climbed all over the monkey bars and swung as high as they could, touching the stars with their toes.

Holly had made a lot of headway on the gingerbread replica of the Page family home today. Throwing herself into showstopper work was a great distraction from the fact that she'd told Danny he was a pathetic dork who sought out other people's approval. When she'd given him the *Harry and the Hendersons* treatment, she'd forgotten about the fact that she still had to text him as Elda. And, thanks to that, she knew exactly how much she'd hurt him by telling him she didn't like him.

Nothing could be further from the truth. He was still the guy with a model's physique and a nerd's soul. Even though Holly knew that she definitely was not the one going on this date, she kept thinking about it as if she were—what she'd wear, what kind of knowledge she'd be able to drop on Danny, whether or not they'd kiss. But it was all in her head. Elda was the one going out with Danny, not her.

"Are you looking forward to your date tomorrow?" Holly asked Elda as they waited in line for free popcorn in the park. A booth had opened up near the big statue of St. Nick, and the queue was already thirty people deep. No one in North Pole could turn down free popcorn.

"Yeah," Elda said. "But I'm nervous."

"That's good," Holly said. "Nerves are good. They mean you're excited."

The smell of popcorn had made its way to Holly's nostrils, and her stomach growled. She hadn't eaten much all day. She'd been too busy working on the showstopper, and she must've really been in the zone.

"I went into Santabucks today," Elda said. "It was... awkward. I wonder if we're going about this all wrong."

"What are you talking about?"

"I mean, Danny and I have nothing to say to each other in person. The only reason he likes me is because of the stuff you've texted him. You've made him think I'm this person who likes architecture and historical non-fiction. I like dead things and plumbing and gross YouTube videos. I have no clue what we're going to talk about."

"Well." Holly wasn't sure what to add. Maybe Elda had a point. Holly probably should've played to Elda's strengths in those text conversations, but this had been all about wooing Danny Garland. He just happened to like the stuff Holly liked. That couldn't be helped. Not many people were interested in watching videos of people snaking shower drains. That was a pretty niche obsession. "Well," she said again, "you have all the texts Danny and I sent to each other on your phone. Just read through those, you know, get familiar with the stuff we discussed. If you want, you and I can go home tonight, and I'll give you a tutorial on architecture and whatever else you need to bone up on—movie references, that sort of thing."

"I've been thinking." Elda pulled her jacket tighter around her waist. The temperature today was mild for Holly and the Minnesotans, but it was basically freezing for Elda, the California girl. "Maybe it's time for me to take over the texting. Maybe it's time for me to start being me."

"Oh." Elda being Elda. Duh. That was what this whole thing had been leading up to, right? To the point where Elda felt comfortable enough to show Danny her true colors? Holly was going to have to get off the phone eventually. But Holly didn't want to get off the phone. "I don't know. Maybe."

"It's almost Christmas," Elda said. "We've got, like, a week left here."

"Yeah?" Dread coiled up Holly's spine.

"And…you've been awesome helping me out with Danny so far, and I'm so grateful to you for opening that door, but… at some point he has to start liking me for me."

Elda was watching the gazebo in the middle of the park, which was being used as a stage. Dinesh was at the microphone, wearing a red, green, and white Elvis costume while belting out "Blue Christmas." Man, North Pole loved karaoke almost as much as it loved Mariah Carey. Elda let out a massive "woot!" for Dinesh and clapped like a very noisy seal.

She was right. Danny deserved to get to know the real Elda, because Elda was great. Yeah, she had some weird interests, but that was part of her charm. If a guy couldn't see that, then he didn't deserve to be with her, even if he was someone as awesome as Danny Garland.

Holly was going to have to *Harry and the Hendersons* her last tether to Danny. For his sake, and Elda's.

Holly placed her hands on her cousin's cheeks and turned

her head away from Dinesh in his sparkly, fitted jumpsuit. "You're absolutely right. You and Danny have to do this on your own. I'm tapping out."

"Tapping out?"

"I'm handing you the reins. Danny Garland deserves to meet the real Elda."

Elda gave Holly a quick hug. "Thank you. I mean, I'm nervous as hell, and I'm not sure how this is going to turn out, but I really need to give it a go."

Holly barely heard her through the ringing in her ears. She was desperately trying to think back to her last conversation with Danny. What had they talked about? Did it have something to do with the Chicago skyline? Maybe. Or food? Was it their discussion of the hierarchy of fast food places while on a road trip? She bit her top lip. It sucked that she couldn't remember. It was unfair. She had to remember. She needed this one thing.

Elda put an arm around Holly's shoulders. "Hey. You okay?"

Holly nodded. "Just thinking about how much work I still have to do on the showstopper."

"You sure that's it?"

"Totally." At least Holly still had that to focus on. And cleaning out her grandma's house. Danny had been a nice distraction, but that was over now. He and Elda were going out on a real date tomorrow, and they were going to be so happy. It was a good thing, for everyone. This was what they'd both wanted from the start.

Elda pulled Holly closer to her side, and the two of them stood in line for popcorn, cheering on Dinesh and his swiveling pelvis.

Chapter Twelve

Friday, December 22

"Dan," Jamison whispered in his ear as she passed by him. He was still perched on his stool behind the counter at the coffee shop, even though his shift was long over. "I was wrong. This girl is rad."

Danny spun halfway around and checked out Elda, who was lying on the floor near the end of the counter, her legs sticking out from under the sink. She was fixing their leaky faucet.

As she slid out from under the cabinet, her shirt went up a bit, revealing a very toned stomach. Yes, Danny noticed, and he definitely noticed Jamison noticing, as well.

"So, you think she's hot now," he whispered as Jamison refilled pitchers with milk and cream at the counter next to him.

Jamison blushed slightly and made a big show of screwing the cap back on the container of half and half. "I never said she wasn't hot. But a girl with a tool belt, I mean, come on."

"Shallow." Danny nudged her in the arm.

Jamison winked. "Maybe I am."

It was the day of his North Pole architecture tour date, and Danny felt a bit like someone was forcing him to eat his vegetables, which was silly. Elda wasn't broccoli. She was a beautiful, nice, friendly girl who knew her way around a p-trap, which was a word he'd learned from Elda five minutes ago. He simply couldn't get over how different she was in person from when they were chatting via text. Elda on the phone knew a lot about history and art and architecture. Elda in real life seemed to only want to talk about her most recent finds in her grandma's garbage disposal.

"You're okay to walk?" Elda asked as the two of them strolled down Main Street.

"Totally fine," Danny lied. He hadn't thought this through when he'd bought the tickets. He'd been so excited about the idea of taking Elda out on the perfect date that he'd forgotten entirely about his leg situation, which was unfortunate, since this was a walking tour. The crutches were horribly annoying and hurt his armpits, but he wouldn't let Elda know that. He'd make it work. At least it was fairly warm outside this afternoon, and the sidewalks were miraculously clear of ice and snow. December had been precipitation free, which was the only tangible proof that maybe the entire universe wasn't conspiring against him.

"You're really good at the plumbing stuff," he said, as the two of them strolled past the video store on the corner, and Danny caught sight of their reflection in the window. They were an attractive couple. He couldn't deny that. They looked like two people who should be together. But appearances could be deceiving.

Elda shot him a shy smile. "My best friend from home, Lexi, her dad's a plumber. She's an only child and has no interest in what he does, but I'd have him show me stuff when

I was over there. Like, Lexi'd be lying on the couch watching TV, and I'd have him teach me how to install a sink. I'm not good at sitting still."

This beautiful girl knew her way around a toolbox. Jamison was right. It was kind of exciting. He could imagine himself telling people about Elda installing a new kitchen sink, and they'd think it was cool. And then Danny'd be cool by association.

And there he was trying to get people to like him again. Damn it. Just like that, Holly was back inside his head.

Elda gestured toward the building to their right, Mags's Diner, one of the oldest storefronts in town. "Did you know that used to be a house?" Elda sounded like she was reciting lines from a play.

"I did, yeah," Danny said.

Elda kept going, as if she'd memorized this monologue and she was going to finish it. "The first settlers in this town lived there, the Bell family. They moved in during the mid-1800s." Now her eyes lit up. "They all died. Right inside the house. From lead poisoning. Their plates and bowls were made out of the lead from the nearby mines."

"I did not know that part," Danny said.

"It's interesting, right?" Elda stared at the building like she could see the ghosts of the Bell family lurking inside.

It was interesting, Danny supposed, but he was more interested in the intricate stonework on the outside walls and the renovations Mags had to do before opening the restaurant—she'd had to lengthen the doorways, for example. People were much shorter back in the day. "I just hope Mags doesn't use those same dishes in her diner."

Elda snorted. "Oh my God! What if she's been using lead plates this whole time and they've affected people's brains, and that's why this place is so Christmas obsessed?"

Danny grinned. This sounded more like the smart,

snarky, imaginative girl he'd been texting for the past few days. "That's a great idea for a movie. I should ask my friend Sam to write the script."

Elda, who had skipped ahead of him a few paces, spun around, and the sunlight reflected off the reddish highlights in her hair. "What's your favorite movie?"

Hadn't they already talked about it? Danny could've sworn that had been part of one of their first conversations. He'd said that he loved *Taxi Driver*, and Elda had said that she was more of a *Goodfellas* girl. Then they got into a discussion about their favorite Martin Scorsese movies. Maybe she'd forgotten. "You talkin' to me?" he said with a grin.

Elda frowned. "Yeah," she said, holding her hand over her eyes to block the sun's glare. She glanced around, scanning the crowds of tourists walking down Main Street. "Who else would I be talking to?"

"No," Danny said. "*Taxi Driver.* Remember. It's my favorite movie. It's a line…Robert De Niro…"

Elda's eyes narrowed, questioning, for a moment. Then she giggled, waving Danny off. "I remember. I was just messing with you."

"Oh. Good joke." But it wasn't, really. It was just kind of odd, and not at all how she would've responded on the phone. Via text, she probably would've asked if Danny thought she was a clown, and she would've included a gif of Joe Pesci with it. But Elda still looked bewildered, like she had no idea what Danny was talking about.

"So, do you really think Holly hates you?" Elda asked as they passed the arcade. She was peeking into the windows.

She was bringing up Holly now? On their date? Holly was the last person Danny wanted to think about today. "Oh. I don't know," Danny said. "I mean, she said she doesn't like me, so."

"Holly can be kind of a tough nut to crack," Elda said.

"For what it's worth, I don't think she hates you. She's just…
Holly." They were past the arcade now, and Elda seemed
to have stopped searching for something outside their
conversation.

"During the second round of the gingerbread competition,
when you weren't there, Holly and I had, I thought, a pretty
good conversation. She's interesting and funny." And cute.
"But then she snapped at me in the arcade later. I don't know
what I did."

"I'm sure you didn't do anything. She's super private
and in her head." Elda touched her temple. "Her snapping
probably had nothing to do with you. Wrong place, wrong
time. She's sad, too. She won't talk about it, but I know she
misses our grandma."

This was one of the longest, easiest conversations he and
Elda'd had in person to date, and it was all about Holly. He
might as well keep it going. "Does she have a boyfriend?"

"Holly?" Elda raised her eyebrows, then she shook her
head. "No. At least I don't think so. We talk all the time,
but she doesn't say much about herself, really. She's always
helping me with my problems. She's a great listener, and she'd
do anything for the people she cares about." Elda frowned,
stopping short on the sidewalk, deep in thought. "I can't say
I know as much about her. Maybe because I don't ask." She
looked right at Danny. "Maybe I should ask."

The two of them walked in silence the rest of the way
down the block.

At the architecture tour office, Craig was standing behind
the front counter in his mom jeans and blue fleece jacket. He
was going to be their tour guide today. Naturally. "What are
you two doing here?"

"We're here for the tour, Craig," Danny said.

"We're on a date." Elda moved a step closer to Danny
and gazed up at him. He considered putting an arm around

her or taking her hand or something else date-like, but none of that felt right to him. Would it be too soon, too forward, too presumptuous? He patted her shoulder instead, which was definitely the wrong move. Ugh.

Craig looked from Danny to Elda and back to Danny. "I don't see it."

"You don't have to see it, Craig." Danny's face flushed. Damn it, Craig, always noticing and commenting on every little thing. Why couldn't he just mind his own business like everyone else?

Craig grabbed his guidebook and led them out onto Main Street. He pointed out the flying buttresses on the chapel and the gorgeous stained-glass windows off the back of The Chinese Restaurant.

But on the way to Prince's Summer Sports, Craig sidled up to Elda. "How long does this date last?"

"I don't know, Craig." Elda raised her eyebrows. "It's a date. It lasts as long as it lasts."

What did she mean by that? Was she saying she'd stick with Danny for as long as they were having some approximation of fun, or that she was booking it out of here the second the tour was over?

"Some of us are meeting up at the arcade later, if you're interested." Craig nodded down the street, toward Santa's Playhouse.

"Okay, Craig. Enough. Just keep talking about the buildings." Danny wedged his body between Craig's and Elda's. He was actually flirting with Danny's date right in front of him. *What the hell, Craig?*

"I...um..." Elda's shoulders were up by her ears. She was the picture of discomfort. "So, what's your favorite building in North Pole?"

"Mags's Diner," Craig said right away.

"Danny," Elda said. "I was asking Danny." She smiled at

Danny, but it didn't reach her eyes. She was only a few inches shorter than him, unlike Holly. He had over a half a foot on Holly.

Danny rolled his eyes at Elda—he wasn't sure why, if it was because this was such an absurd date or because he was feeling uncomfortable, but whatever. Why didn't matter. It made her laugh. And then he was laughing, too. He felt better than he had all day. He'd been so tense, which was silly. He was on a date with this awesome girl who liked him, whom he liked, too. He had to stop worrying about saying the right thing or whether or not Craig had more game than he did. All that mattered right now was Elda. "I love the town hall," he said.

She was still watching him, brow furrowed.

Craig, who had been attempting to describe the brickwork on Prince's Summer Sports, folded his arms. "I'll wait, while you finish your obviously very important conversation."

Danny's heart sped up a bit as he told Elda his story and tried to block out Craig's angry glare. "I remember back when we were kids, you and your grandma built this replica of the North Pole Town Hall, and it was, I think, my favorite gingerbread showstopper of all time. You captured the essence of the place, but with licorice columns and lollipop trees and steps made of marzipan. I remember looking at it and being like, I want to live there." He grinned down at her. "Whenever I see the town hall, I think about that showstopper. And... well...you." Now he knew he was blushing. It was the most real he'd gotten with Elda in person. If Craig hadn't been standing right next to them, this probably would've been the time for them to kiss.

Danny waited for Elda's reaction. She had to give him something—a smile, a nod, a squeeze of the hand, some acknowledgement that this was a big moment for the two of them.

But she stayed lost in her own world. Her face wasn't relieved or happy or excited or any of the emotions Danny had been banking on. She looked sad, actually. She looked like the admission about her town hall showstopper was the worst possible thing he could've said. That probably had something to do with Danny making the rookie mistake of bringing up a girl's recently deceased grandmother on a date.

Danny, attempting to move on, asked Craig, "What about the brickwork?" And their tour continued, though Danny blocked out every single word. He couldn't get Elda's frown out of his head.

Outside the bakery, Craig talked about how the building used to be a haberdashery back in the day. Elda's arms were folded, and she kept looking off to the side, like she wasn't listening to any of it. This date was a failure. Danny was a failure. He'd opened up to Elda, and it had been exactly the wrong thing to do. He had shown her a bit of who he was, and she'd rejected him.

When he was with Star, he was always altering his opinions or hiding his true feelings because of her. After they broke up, he vowed not to get into another relationship like that, but maybe that was just how relationships worked and making concessions was all part of the deal. Maybe if Elda wasn't going to come to him, he'd have to meet her where she was. At least that'd give him a fighting chance.

"That's very cool, Craig." Danny had no actual idea what he'd been talking about, but that was pretty much standard when it came to his interactions with Craig. Danny peered into the front window of the bakery. Tinka was inside decorating a tray of cookies. "All the architecture info is great, but what I really want to know is: what's the grossest stuff that's ever happened in this town? Where are the literal bodies buried?"

Elda was looking at him now, a faint and curious smile on her face. She reached over and squeezed his hand, which was clutching the handle of his crutch. His body warmed slightly, though he felt like he'd only won the battle, not the war. Things were still kind of odd. She'd frowned at him when he confessed that he'd been thinking about her for years, but she was ready with a hand squeeze at the first mention of dead bodies.

They walked next to each other down Main Street, listening to Craig tell stories about the skeleton that was found under the roof above the Mexican restaurant, and the teenage girl who was hit by a car back in the 1930s and still haunted the gun shop, and the alleged half man-half goat who used to live in the apartment above the dry cleaners. Elda grinned and cheered and squealed as Craig revealed every scandalous detail.

Danny could barely muster a smile. This girl in person was so different from the girl whose words had been all over his phone screen for the past week or so. He'd built their budding romance into something perfect—a neat, precise structure that had met every one of his specifications. But life wasn't perfect, and neither were people. He wasn't being fair to Elda, expecting her to conform to this specific little image he'd created in his head.

When the tour finally ended, Danny, whose left leg was about to fall off from overuse, took off toward home with Elda.

"This was fun." Elda did a little twirl on the sidewalk. "Thanks." She beamed as the two of them walked down the street. "Those stories Craig told." Her eyes sparkled. "I love that stuff, don't you?"

He didn't, but he liked that she liked it. The fact that Elda was into some creepy stuff made her interesting. "Yeah, sure. I totally love it."

Elda stopped walking and narrowed her eyes at him. "Liar." Her hands were on her hips, and she was staring at him hard.

He stopped, too, and leaned on his crutches. He needed a long nap or something. He was physically and emotionally drained from this afternoon. "No, I really like this stuff," he said, plastering on a big smile. "If it doesn't seem like it, I'm just beat."

She nodded slowly, and Danny got the sense that she still didn't believe him. "If you say so." She was testing him.

"I do say so." He started walking again, and so did she.

"Well, since you're all in on this creepy supernatural North Pole stuff, then I bet you've gone looking for some things, like the goat man."

"You actually believe there's a goat man?" he asked.

"Don't you?"

Danny was a total cynic. He'd lived here his entire life, and he'd heard all the stories before. He'd never once seen a ghost or a goat man or even a ghost of a goat. He'd assumed Elda was just like him. The girl he'd been texting with had come off as pragmatic as he was. She would've been able to see through all of Craig's bologna. She probably would've been right next to him making jokes about it. Or maybe Danny had misread her earnest words as sarcasm. It was hard to interpret tone in a text message.

Again Danny met Elda where she was instead of dragging her over to his pessimistic side. It's the same way he would've acted with Star, saying what she wanted to hear instead of voicing his own opinion. Evidently he was going to have to keep doing this for his entire dating life. "Remember how you fooled me by saying you didn't remember my favorite movie? I was just trying to fool you by pretending the goat man wasn't real," he said. "He totally is. The goat man graduated from high school with my mom, actually."

Elda folded her arms, watching him again. "I know you're kidding," she said. "But I'm going to pretend you're not because it's more fun that way."

Danny followed Elda down the street. He was never, ever going to find someone who totally got him. He'd keep working his ass off to understand others, but no one was ever going to try to understand him.

. . .

Holly's gingerbread replica of her grandma's house was really taking shape. And it was a great distraction from the fact that Elda and Danny were out on their date right now. The baking was done, and she'd moved on to constructing the showstopper out in the garage. By herself. Away from people, just the way she liked it.

But Holly wasn't completely alone. Her grandmother was with her. Holly sensed her presence in the air. This was what she was meant to do. She was supposed to recreate this house that had meant so much to Grandma and Holly and the rest of the family. They were about to hand the keys over to someone new, and this would be Holly's last opportunity to honor their past, to show the entire town what this place had meant to all of them.

She was just adhering the turreted roof when Elda came in, wearing a pair of old jeans from when Aunt Vixi was in high school and an oversize men's undershirt. She waved and went right over to Grandma's workbench, hunting for tools.

Holly checked her watch. Almost six. "How was your date?"

"Um...fine."

"Fine?" Was that really all she had to say? Maybe it was enough. Holly's mind was stuck between wanting to know and wanting to run away screaming with her fingers in her ears.

Elda slammed a drawer shut. "I've got to go to the

hardware store."

"What for?"

Elda wrapped an old tool belt around her waist and threw her long, dark hair up in a ponytail. "Pipe dope and water-pump pliers. The valve seat in the bathroom sink is rough."

Holly only understood about half the words in that statement. With her life on the line, Holly would have no idea where to start on a sink. She'd probably flood the whole house. Her parents were terrified of pipes and drains and faucets. Holly's dad had never attempted anything more difficult than unclogging a drain.

Elda came over and crouched down next to Holly, hiking those baggy jeans up over her slender hips. "Wow. This is really coming together." Elda ran a hand over the turret's cone-shaped roof. "How'd you even do this?"

Holly was super proud of the roof. While baking the walls of the house, she'd hemmed and hawed about how to do the turret. Then she found a can in the recycling bin, around which she baked the rounded wing of the house. Then she used a scrap of sheet metal from the garage to form the mold for the cone-shaped roof. It turned out perfectly on the first try, like Holly had experienced divine baking intervention. Thanks, Grandma.

Elda picked up one of the tiny gingerbread fence posts Holly had been working on earlier. An actual gingerbread house wasn't the sexiest, most out-of-the-box idea, but she was going to create such a perfect replica no one would be able to accuse her of taking the easy way out. "I'm impressed."

"Hopefully the judges will be, too." Holly wiped her sticky hands on a wet towel and grabbed a sip of water from the "World's Best Grandma" mug. "So, please, tell me about your date." She didn't really want to hear, but she had to know.

Elda popped a gumdrop in her mouth, and Holly swatted

her hand away from the bowl. She needed every last piece for this showstopper. "Like I said, it was fine. I just...I don't know if we're compatible."

"Sure you are," Holly said. "You could be the king and queen of North Pole."

Elda pulled up a chair next to Holly's at the table. "He's pretending to like the things I like."

Holly shrugged. "That's how it works, right? You pretend to like the stuff he likes, he pretends to like the stuff you like, and by the time you figure out you have nothing in common, it's too late."

Elda laughed. "Tell me you're kidding."

"I'm kind of kidding," Holly said. "But, like, isn't it all about putting your best foot forward to make a good impression? Isn't that the game?" In her own case, Holly was putting her cousin's face forward, since it was such a good face. Elda, as awkward as she was, drew people to her. Holly, the loner, didn't.

"I'm starting to think it should be easier, like, I want a guy to like me for me. Isn't that what you want?"

I'd like a guy to like me at all, *thanks.*

Elda picked up the little marzipan figure of herself. "The only time our conversation really clicked was when we were talking about you."

Holly folded her arms and gazed over at her cousin. "Stop."

"I mean it. He was all, 'Holly hates me. What did I do?' Maybe you should date him."

Holly giggled. She should date him. Yeah, right. Maybe in some universe that didn't even exist yet. Her nervous laugh was nearly out of control right from the start. When she was finally able to control herself, she said, "You're out of your gourd. Don't be ridiculous."

"I'm not being ridiculous. You're the one who's had all

these meaningful chats with him on my phone. I mean, you two text for *hours*. Hours, Holly. He bought the architecture tour tickets to impress the girl he thought would appreciate them."

"He bought them because he thought he was talking to you."

"Okay, I just spent the afternoon with him, and he was not impressed by me. Not even a bit. But he's all concerned that you don't like him. Which I don't think is true at all. I think you do like him. Very much."

Holly rolled her eyes. Oh my God, this conversation. Elda had to get off this topic. If people started talking about Holly liking Danny, holy crap, she'd be mortified. She'd be dead. She'd literally not survive the next ten days. "Do I think Danny's cute? Sure. But who doesn't? He's universally attractive."

"And you think he's smart and nice. The two of you have a lot in common."

"And we have one very, very glaring difference—we are not even remotely in the same league. He's, like, Mr. Super Celebrity, King of Popularity around here, and I'm hiding from the world in my grandma's garage."

"Stop selling yourself short."

"I'm not, Elda. I'm valuating myself at exactly the right price." Her hand twitched involuntarily. She hadn't texted Danny in over twenty-four hours, and she was jonesing for a fix. Building the gingerbread showstopper was great, but it couldn't hold a candle to chatting with her crush, the guy whom she was trying desperately to hand over to her cousin, if only she would take him. "Someone like Danny Garland would never, ever go for a girl like me. Not that I want him to. I don't like Danny, so let's stop talking about this, oh my God."

"Okay." Elda hoisted herself up from the floor.

"Hey," Holly said, "you want to run with me out to Wal-Mart in the morning to find more candy?"

Elda shrugged. "Sure. Early?"

"Early," Holly said. "Like eight?"

"Perfect. And Holly, one more thing. Danny and I were together all day today. He didn't even try to make a move on me. He patted my shoulder once." She laughed.

So did Holly, because who patted a shoulder?

"If he was just looking for a meaningless fling with a pretty girl, he would've tried harder today." She raised her eyebrows all the way to her hairline, as if that was supposed to complete her thought.

It did. "Point made," Holly said. "Even though none of this has anything to do with my situation. I don't like Danny. And he doesn't like me." He liked Elda, he wanted Elda, and Holly would never crush his soul by telling him she'd been the one behind those texts.

Seeing the disappointment in his eyes would ruin her.

Chapter Thirteen

ELDA: *Hey.*

DANNY: *Hi!*

ELDA: *I'm running out to Wal-Mart tomorrow morning. For candy. Want to come?*

DANNY: *Okay.*

ELDA: *8 AM. I'll pick you up at Santabucks.*

DANNY: *See you then!*

DANNY: *(gif of De Niro from Taxi Driver)*

DANNY: *(gif of Joe Pesci from Goodfellas)*

DANNY: *(gif of someone screaming into the abyss)*

DANNY: *(gif of someone else screaming into the abyss)*

DANNY: *(gif of a skeleton staring at his phone, waiting for a response)*

Chapter Fourteen

Saturday, December 23

"She'll be here," Jamison said. "Stop worrying."

"Whatever." Danny was sitting at one of the Santabucks tables, waiting for Elda to show up. They were supposed to be going shopping together for extra showstopper supplies, but she was five minutes late. He was picturing a whole slew of scenarios right now—she'd found something unsavory about him online and had lost interest, she'd stopped responding to his texts last night because she'd had a heart attack or someone else had had a heart attack, she was somewhere in North Pole right now making out with Phil Waterston...

An unfamiliar light-blue minivan pulled up outside, and Danny perked up. Elda wasn't blowing him off. Well, that was progress. Two doors opened, and two girls hopped out. Elda and Holly. *Holly.* Danny's emotions were such a mess of confusion, he dropped half his cinnamon crunch muffin on the floor.

The little bell over the door jingled as they entered, and

Holly scanned the room. Her eyes stopped on Danny for a moment, but she looked away as fast as it happened. So did he. He leaned down to pick up his breakfast from the coffee shop floor. He had no idea what to say to her at this point, or why he should bother saying anything at all. She was just a tourist in town for Christmas. He owed her nothing. What did it matter if she thought he was a needy loser? Making small talk would only serve to highlight his puppy dog nature.

"Hey." He waved specifically to Elda.

She ran over and squeezed his shoulder. "Hey."

Holly, barely glancing at him, went to the counter and ordered a mocha to go.

"You excited to go to Wal-Mart?" Elda asked.

"Is anyone ever?" Danny said with a grin.

She nudged him in the arm as her phone buzzed. "Oh, shoot," she said after reading the text. She frowned and looked Danny right in the eye. "It's Dinesh. Apparently he, well, I don't want to get into the gory details, but there's a sink-related emergency over at the arcade, and he totally needs my help." She glanced over at Holly. "I'm sorry, guys. I have to deal with this." She waved her phone in the air. He saw an actual text from Dinesh on her screen. She was telling the truth.

"We can wait for you," Danny said.

Holly glared at her cousin. "Yeah," she said. "We have all day."

"No, you don't." Elda already had one foot out the door. "And this thing with Dinesh could take hours. Like, literally hours. Go on without me." The bell jingled, and she was gone.

No Elda. No buffer. Just Danny, Holly, and a minivan.

"I really do need to buy more candy," she said.

"Me, too." He kept staring at the door, trying to name all the feelings swirling around in his stomach right now. Dread was there, for sure, and annoyance. But also kind of maybe a hint of excitement.

Holly walked over and placed her to-go cup on the table. She bit her upper lip with her lower teeth. And Danny was able to identify another emotion: desire. God, she was cute. Too bad she thought he was the most pathetic person in all of North Pole. "So, are you ready?" she said.

Danny shook his head. "You don't have to. I'll get my brother to drive me later."

"Don't be silly. Let's go." Holly picked up her cup and went to the door, which she held open for him.

He took a deep breath and dragged himself up from his chair. A whole morning alone with Holly. This day was going to end in tears—his. Still, he followed her out to the minivan. Holly grabbed his crutches and tossed them into the back.

"Thanks." Most people didn't offer to help him. He wasn't sure if people just felt awkward about it or if they thought offering to help might offend him. Maybe they figured he was a young, healthy guy with a broken leg, and he could handle himself. They were right about that, for the most part. Danny could handle himself, but it was nice of Holly to show him the courtesy.

"What do you need at the store?" Holly turned the key in the ignition.

"I think, like, M&Ms or something else colorful. I'm building a basketball court, and I want to fill in the stands with little candies." Already they were talking about things Danny was interested in. Why couldn't it be this easy with Elda? Maybe because his relationship with Holly was never going to be more than a reluctant friendship. They weren't trying to impress each other, so they could talk about anything, even stuff as mundane as making candy people for his gingerbread showstopper.

Holly squinted as she pulled onto Main Street. "Jelly beans, maybe? More colors. More variations. The M&Ms might come off too same-y."

"Good point." She was dead right. "You've really gotten to know your stuff over the past week."

She blushed. "Gingerbread boot camp, I don't know." Her hands kneaded the steering wheel. "Building a basketball court is a really cool idea. I can't wait to see it."

Danny suppressed a grin. Deep down—maybe not so deep down—he was just a sad nerd who needed to be liked. Maybe he should stop trying to fight it.

"How was your date with Elda yesterday?" Holly peeked at him out of the corner of her eye.

"All right." Danny watched the bobblehead Bears player on the dashboard move in rhythm to Holly's driving. She and Elda had to have talked about the date. Elda had probably told Holly how badly it went, and now Holly was preparing to rub it in. "You mind if I roll the window down?" Without waiting for an answer, he pressed the button and closed his eyes as the cold air whipped his face.

"You like Elda, right?" Holly said. "Like, I mean, you *like*-like her."

"Elda's great." Danny spoke into the wind. "I just wish things could click easier between us in person. I don't know if we're both just super awkward or what." He'd avoided the actual question. *Like*-like was such a strong word.

"Elda is really awkward around the guys she likes, if that helps."

Hey, Holly wasn't rubbing his inability to properly woo her cousin in his face. That was something. "I think it does. I mean, I'm totally out of practice with this whole dating thing, myself."

"Maybe the two of you just need to jump in with both feet," Holly said, "Stop waiting for the right moment or for things to get less awkward. Just go for it."

This whole thing with Elda was driving him batty. He wasn't sure which way was up and which was down. Even though their date had been only okay, she still asked him to hang out after it. But then she blew him off for Dinesh this morning. Frankly, Danny didn't really want to talk about the date anymore.

The one good part of their conversation, the only time they really clicked yesterday, was when they talked about how Holly never volunteered information about herself. He didn't want to be the guy who only talked about his own problems. "Can I ask you something?"

Holly shrugged, staring at the road in front of them.

"How did you actually get that scar?"

She immediately covered her mouth. "I thought I told you." She lowered her hand, trying to give off the illusion of cool. "Street fight."

"Come on. What's the real story? I'm not just trying to be nice or get you to like me. I actually want to know." Danny was being pushy. He backed off. "I mean, if you want to talk about it. You don't have to." The scar was just a tiny thing, but the fact that she'd been all cagey about how she got it, had been gnawing at Danny for days. A story lived behind her fib, and Danny needed to know Holly's stories.

She clutched and unclutched the steering wheel a few times. "All right. I'll tell you. It's not a big deal, really. A dog bit me."

"No way." Danny craned his neck to see the scar better, but she scooted away and ducked her head, like that was her default response.

She caught herself, though, and turned slightly toward Danny while keeping her eyes on the road, giving him the full view. It was a small scar, really, a white line going from her nose down her upper lip. "It was my dog, actually."

Danny pointed to her collarbone, where he knew a dog tattoo was hiding under her chunky cardigan. "The tattoo."

"The tattoo." Holly bit her lip again, caught herself, and

let her mouth relax.

"What happened?" He had to keep her talking, like back when they were working on their gingerbread houses next to each other. He wanted that banter back. Talking to Holly, and it was silly to think this, but it almost gave him the same rush as when he was texting Elda.

"Oh, it was ridiculous." Holly shook her head. "The dog was on the couch eating a pig ear, and I should've known better than to bother her, but I leaned down and kissed her head." Holly shrugged. "She didn't growl or anything. She gave me no warning. One second my lips were on her fur, the next, she'd taken a chunk out of my face."

"Oh shit." Danny touched his own lip. "What did you do then?"

"It seems so ridiculous, but I ran up to the bathroom and checked the mirror. It looked like someone had shot a bullet through my lip." She pressed on the scar. "There was blood running down my nose from where she'd clipped me up here, too." Holly touched the side of her nose, right near the edge of her eyebrow. "She'd missed my eye by, like, half an inch."

"When did this happen?"

"Like two days before the start of freshman year, which is kind of hilarious because I'd had this huge plan to show up at school looking fabulous, ready to take the world by storm. Instead, I had a massive, gross, oozing wound on my face." She laughed. "Elda probably would've loved it."

"Totally." Danny winced. Elda. What did she have to do with any of this?

"The thing ended up on my school I.D. for the entire year, and I became known as Rabies Girl. Hooray."

"Jackasses." What kinds of human garbage would do that to somebody? Not only had Holly been attacked by a dog, but she also had to endure name calling and bullying because of it.

She shrugged. "It's fine. I've been living as Rabies Girl for four years now. Just hoping I don't get mauled by a bear or anything right before college. I'd like to have a fighting chance there."

"The scar's barely noticeable," Danny said.

"It was the first thing you noticed about me."

"Not because it's gross or anything, but because it's interesting...cute." Danny's face warmed, and he faced the window again. "I kind of get where you're coming from, though. I mean, not the bullying or whatever, but," he gestured to his leg, "I had big plans, too."

"Yeah, how did your thing happen?"

"Apparently you don't read the *Minneapolis Star-Tribune*."

She shook her head quickly. "Nope. Sure don't."

"The reporter showed up to interview me about the upcoming season because our team had a chance to win state. Still does, I guess. All these colleges were looking at me. I had a shot at breaking state records. Everything I'd been dreaming about since I was a kid was right at my fingertips. But on a dare, I went up for a dunk and—*crack*."

Holly winced. "Sounds like you and I should stop making plans."

"We're doomed to fail. The future is one big wasteland of disappointment and uncertainty."

Holly pulled into a parking spot and turned off the engine. "I figured you for an optimist, Danny Garland. I like this edgier side of you."

"You said you like me." Danny raised his hands in victory. "I totally made up that story to get you to stop hating me. I can't believe it worked."

Holly eyed him for a second. "You're full of shit."

"Guilty."

She grinned at Danny, pulling her lip into a sly, crooked

smile that was way more than cute.

• • •

"I mean, it's terrible. Infuriating. You have to see it to believe it." Holly leaned back to assess her work. Her showstopper was nearly finished, and she was confident that she had never made anything more beautiful in her life.

Danny was working at a card table a few feet away. After they'd gone shopping, he had Brian wheel over his showstopper on an old wagon so he and Holly could keep each other company while working on their showstoppers. It had been his idea. What was she supposed to tell him? No? She made up some garbage story that Elda had asked her to work on the marzipan figures of their family members. It wasn't a bad lie. Holly was a sculptor after all.

Danny had been trying to force this renewed friendship all day, and Holly had to admit it was kind of working. She liked spending time with him, talking to him, and she was doing a bang-up job of ignoring her more intense feelings for him.

"Of all the things to be angry about in the world, this seems kind of small potatoes," he said. "That's all I'm saying."

Holly added a bit more royal icing to the railing along the front steps. "Maybe I'm so focused on it because I should be pissed about a trillion other, more important things in this messed up world, but the terrible makeup on *Riverdale* is something tangible I can really wrap my head around."

"Okay, I can respect that." Danny smiled at her.

"What about you?" Holly touched her cheek, which was at least five degrees warmer than her hands right now. "What makes you angry?"

Danny leaned back in his chair, surveying his handiwork. His basketball court was definitely coming along. It was super detailed and about the size of large microwave. His idea to shellac the floor with some kind of sugar/gelatin concoction was genius. "You want to know what really gets my goat? Christian Laettner hate."

"What?" Holly laughed. "And also, who?"

Danny gawked at her and dropped one of his jelly-bean spectators to the floor. "You don't know who Christian Laettner is?"

Holly shook her head. "Should I?"

"He's, like, one of the best college basketball players of all time. Full stop."

"Cool. Where does he go to school?"

"Oh my God." Danny buried his face in his hands.

"What?" Holly shrugged.

He looked up. His hands had messed up his usually perfect hair, which was definitely adorable, no matter how hard Holly tried not to notice. "He was in college, like thirty years ago. He played for Duke. Everybody thought he was this rich kid, spoiled baby, but it was all based on assumptions, because, well, he looked like a rich kid, spoiled baby." He pointed a candy cane at Holly. "Before you leave town, we're watching the 'I Hate Christian Laettner' *30 for 30.*"

"You just said a bunch of words that make no sense." Though she definitely heard the part where he mentioned wanting to watch something together.

"Trust me."

"Okay." Grinning like a dork, she focused again on her gingerbread concoction.

"You're seriously not bad." Danny nodded toward her replica of Grandma's house. "I know Elda's the brains behind the operation, but you've got skills, too."

Holly had been avoiding saying Elda's name all day, but now it was out in the open. "She taught me everything I know."

"Well, then you're a fast learner." Danny pulled himself

up from his chair and hopped over to the table where they kept all the extra candy. He was quiet over there, and it took all her will power to keep from looking at him. Holly pulled a bit of marzipan off a block and started molding it into a soft, sticky sphere. This would be her dad's head. She had only four family members to go. "I'd better be careful making my Aunt Vixi," she said. "I'll be in for a world of hurt if my sculpture of her ends up unflattering."

She glanced up, because Danny didn't say anything. He was no longer hunting for the perfect piece of candy. Now he was flipping through a book—Holly's sketch pad.

Shit. She couldn't let him see her most recent sketches.

Her legs immediately tried to push her up, but she stopped herself. He didn't know the book was hers. He'd think it was Elda's, and it would continue the narrative that Elda was the perfect girl for him. If he saw the pictures and knew Holly had made them, he'd book it out of here faster than Elda had ditched them at Santabucks that morning.

"Did you see these drawings?"

Holly shook her head. A ball had formed in her throat, blocking her ability to form words.

Danny tucked the book under one armpit and jumped over to her. He dropped the book in front of Holly and rested his hands on the table next to her.

She kept rolling little marzipan balls. It was all she could do.

Resting one hand on the table for balance, he flipped through the pages. There was a sketch of young Danny at one of the gingerbread contests. And a few more of Danny now. He stopped on one Holly'd made a few days ago, one of him working hard piping icing on his gingerbread figures.

"Wow," Holly said, "so she's been drawing pictures of you. Is that…creepy?" She couldn't read Danny's expression, but of course he wouldn't think it was creepy. He liked Elda.

They'd been on a date, and Elda thinking about him like that was totally legit.

"Maybe I've been making something out of nothing," Danny said.

"What do you mean?"

"I've been worried that Elda doesn't like me, but this kind of proves she does, doesn't it?"

It proved nothing, because those were Holly's sketches, not Elda's. "It's like I told you. She's just awkward around the guys she likes."

"Yeah." Danny flipped through the book one more time, then shut it. "It's just we have so much chemistry when we're—"

"Texting." She looked him straight in the eye.

Danny frowned as he held her gaze. Holly was tempted to look away, but she held on. God, was she really about to do this? She had done such a good job of avoiding embarrassment and hiding her feelings, and now here she was about to ruin it all by letting him see that maybe she enjoyed his company a little bit.

"Are you going to the skating thing later tonight?" she asked.

"The figure skating competition?" he asked. "Planning on it."

"Well, so are we. I mean, so am I. I have to. It's in my grandma's day planner." She played with another ball of marzipan, kneading it to temper her anxiety. "I don't know. Maybe we can hang out."

"You and me?"

"Yeah."

Danny raised his eyebrows.

Holly squeezed the marzipan ball so hard, she squished it like a grape. "I don't know," she said. "Maybe you're not so bad."

Chapter Fifteen

Danny's stomach was in knots, and he wasn't sure why. He and Holly had made plans to meet here at the indoor ice rink for the amateur skating competition tonight. As friends. At least he thought they were meeting as friends. She'd basically only just admitted to him that she didn't think he was abjectly terrible, so Danny was pretty sure she hadn't jumped straight from disgust to desire. Still, he was excited to see her. He'd actually put on some of Brian's cologne, which he was regretting.

Way to be obvious, Garland.

He rubbed his scarf against his neck, trying to wipe off some of the telltale scent.

Danny, sitting in the first row of the bleachers, watched as person after person flew by him on the ice—Dinesh, Sam, Tinka, Marcus, Kevin. Phil Waterston was skating hand in hand with some sophomore girl from the JV basketball team, while Star stayed near her girlfriends, talking a mile a minute and shooting dirty looks at Phil every chance she got.

Danny waved to Dinesh as he exited the rink and barreled

toward the lobby, wobbling on his skates as he made his way across the padded floor. Danny glanced at the clock. It was already a quarter to eight. Holly should've been here by now. He was even more nervous about her whereabouts than he had been when Elda was late this morning. He would've been sad if Elda hadn't shown up at Santabucks, but he'd be devastated if Holly blew him off tonight.

Someone held a hot cup of cocoa in front of his face. Danny spun around. Holly stood there, grinning down at him. He smiled back automatically, without even thinking about it, and the fog in his mind lifted. His entire body flooded with relief. "Hey." He took the cup from her.

Holly sat next to him and dropped her rented skates to the floor. "Elda's here, too. She's talking to Dinesh."

Elda? Who cares about Elda? Danny nodded toward the rink. "So, you're going out there?" *Say no. Don't leave me alone here.*

"Maybe for a minute before the competition starts." Holly tucked some hair behind her ear. She was wearing dangly Christmas tree earrings.

Danny pointed to his own ear.

Holly blushed. "My grandma's. Elda and I raided her jewelry box." Holly glanced back at the lobby. "Where the heck did she go?"

"She'll get here when she gets here." He popped the lid off his hot cocoa and closed his eyes as he inhaled the heady, chocolaty aroma. "This is from Mags's Diner, isn't it?"

Holly nodded.

"She makes the best cocoa in town, but don't tell my mom that."

"Guess what." Holly's hands clutched her knees, and her face was bright with excitement. "You're not going to believe this."

"Try me."

"Okay, what's that thing called when you hear a new word and then all of a sudden it's, like, everywhere?" Her glasses had slipped down her nose, and she pushed them up.

Danny shook his head. "I've heard about this, but I don't know what it's called."

She waved him off. "I'd assumed the guy who had 'philtrum' on the tip of his tongue might know. Anyway." She reached into her bag and pulled out a magazine. "After you left this afternoon, I went up to my grandma's attic and started going through her old magazines. She and my grandpa saved everything, which at first I was kind of annoyed by, but then I started thinking about taking a bunch home to use in collages and stuff. So before tossing them in the recycling bin, I started flipping through the ones that looked interesting, to see if there might be anything worth using."

Danny craned his neck to see what magazine she was holding.

Finally, she turned it around. It was a *People* from 1992. A kind of familiar-looking woman was on the cover, someone famous, he couldn't remember who.

"The most beautiful people of the year," Danny said.

"Exactly." She flipped to a page she had bookmarked with a Post-it Note. "Look who made the cut." She held the pages open for Danny to see. "Christian Laettner."

"Hey." He grabbed the magazine. It was from right after Duke had won the NCAA tournament against Kentucky, after Laettner had put up "the shot" that won the game. It was the kind of sports moment every young athlete dreamed of experiencing at some point in his or her career. Danny and his brother had recreated this shot many, many times in their driveway—with the two of them taking turns playing Laettner and Grant Hill. The shot had put Laettner on the map. It made him a legend, a pop-culture icon. "I remember this picture from that documentary I was telling you about."

Holly snatched the magazine back and gazed into Laettner's bedroom eyes. "You didn't tell me he was a fox."

"I'm sorry I left that part out."

She looked up at him, appraising.

"What?" Danny's eyes narrowed.

So did Holly's. "Nothing."

"I don't look like him, if that's what you were going to say." Danny ran a hand through his hair, which was, admittedly, kind of Laettner-like, though that hadn't been on purpose. That was genetics.

"No, no, not exactly." She glanced down at the page, and then up at him again. "It's the nose. You both have that arrow nose pointing down at your lips." She choked a little on the word "lips."

Danny's hand went to his mouth. "Stop." He couldn't help smiling, though he fought it hard. Holly had noticed his lips.

"I only noticed because I'm an artist, and that's what artists do, obviously. We notice things."

"Of course." Now Danny was about to choke. He was such a glutton for punishment. This same electricity was completely absent whenever he was with Elda. Holly was the Page girl he should be spending time with, no matter how great his texts with Elda had been, no matter how unsure he was of Holly's feelings for him. He had to give this a shot.

"Hey." Danny was about to ask out a girl for the second time in a week. It was no less terrifying, especially since this was the cousin of the first girl he'd asked out, and he wasn't sure about protocol. Still, this chemistry was too good to deny. He knew she was leaving in a little over a week, and this was a time-sensitive matter. If he waited much longer, Holly'd be out of his life for good. Forever. "The video store is showing *Love, Actually* the day after Christmas—"

"Ooh!" Holly's eyes widened, and she cut him off. "Elda

and I love that movie." She glanced toward the lobby and waved over Elda, who was carrying two big bags of popcorn. "We totally have to go."

• • •

Holly had choked.

She'd cut Danny off before he could finish whatever he was about to say. In those split seconds, she'd seen every possible outcome—*Love, Actually* was playing at the video store and he wanted to ask Elda out again, or maybe he'd wanted to go with Holly just as friends, or, completely unlikely, he was asking Holly out on a date. That terrified her more than the other possibilities, honestly. For one thing, she'd have to clear it with Elda first, out of courtesy. For another, Holly had spent the past week or so deceiving Danny. She had misrepresented herself to him since day one. If she went out with him, she'd have to come clean with him at some point, and she wouldn't blame him if he couldn't forgive her for that.

But they could hang out as friends. "Friends" she could do. Buddies who hung out and never, ever got to the point where they had to discuss the awful, deceitful way she and Elda had kicked off their relationship with Danny.

Holly waved over Elda and Dinesh and scooted toward the middle of the bench to make room for the two of them between herself and Danny. She needed space. Dinesh, who was right next to her, handed Holly a box of popcorn. Here they were, a quartet on a weird sort of double date.

"Did you get the sink fixed?" Holly asked.

"Sure did," Dinesh said. "Elda's a pro."

Elda beamed at him.

Thankfully, that was when the figure skating competition started.

After watching a world championship competition on

TV when she was about six, Holly had started to fancy herself a figure skater. They made it look so easy. She'd go down to her basement and perform routines set to, like, the overture from *Jesus Christ Superstar* or whatever.

She'd come back to North Pole the next Christmas ready to wow everyone with her amazing skills. She'd lace up her skates and wobble out onto the ice, where she'd promptly fall down. She'd get up and fall down again. The routine she'd performed so effortlessly at home on her basement floor was impossible on the ice.

That was the first time Holly understood that just dreaming about something didn't make it so. Her imagination sustained her. Trying to reach beyond that had always, predictably, ended in disappointment.

Holly was going to be in North Pole for a little over a week. She could dump all her feelings on Danny and face rejection, or she could hang back, be cool, and let their friendship continue to bloom. In one scenario, she'd get to see Danny, to joke with him and work on their gingerbread showstoppers together. In the other, she'd ruin everything and scare him away.

Friendship was safe and predictable. She understood the rules. The sweet agony she felt every time she was in the room with him was familiar to her. That she could live with.

Holly glanced down the row. Danny and Elda were chatting, completely engrossed in what the other was saying. Holly focused on the ice. She'd pushed them back together. Good. That's the way it was supposed to be, never mind the lump growing in her throat right now.

Sam, Tinka, and Craig had taken the row behind them. Sam's little sister, Maddie, was actually living Holly's childhood dream of figure skating stardom. She was only nine years old but could do these amazing spins and jumps that Holly could barely do, even on solid ground.

"She practices every day," Sam said. "She gets up at five in the morning to come here before school, then a few hours after school, too. My dad's constantly driving her to competitions all over the place."

Holly watched as Maddie twirled like a top in the center of the ice before abruptly stopping and raising an arm with a flourish. Her chest heaved as she gazed up at the ceiling with a content smile. Then she bowed to the judges and waved to her brother before skating off to the side as the lights caught every sequin on her short purple dress.

Maybe that was a big part of the reason Holly had always wanted to be a figure skater—the shiny clothes. She was such a magpie.

After the awards had been handed out and Maddie had won first place in the youth group, Holly dashed alone out into the lobby and tossed her unused skates up on the counter. She'd get out of here fast, go home, and finish her showstopper for tomorrow. Her foot tapped on the floor as she waited for her shoes.

Danny came through the door, still talking to Elda. Holly averted her eyes. God, these two certainly had enough to say to each other tonight.

"Hey, Garland," some guy shouted. His voice boomed so loud that everyone turned to look. The guy was pointing all the way across the room to the ceiling above Danny's head. "You're under the mistletoe."

An entire scenario flew through Holly's imagination in a split second. She pictured doing the bold thing, the thing she'd only ever do in her head, marching all the way across the room and kissing him right in front of everyone. Her mini-daydream ended with a "happily ever after," because that's how daydreams were supposed to end.

"Someone kiss Danny already," the same guy announced to the crowd.

Danny's eyes met Holly's over at the skate return. That really happened. Some dude said the word "kiss" and Danny had looked at Holly. Her heart sped up, excited, wanting to believe this was real, that her dream was actually coming true.

But then Danny frowned. He winced. It was a look Holly knew well, one she was used to seeing.

That was the danger of dreaming. It was just a way to escape reality until it came full force and slammed the unsuspecting dreamer into a wall. The reality was that Danny would push her away if she tried to kiss him. He'd reject her, possibly even laugh at her, in public, and she'd be subjected to yet another version of "I'm not that into you." She couldn't handle hearing that right now, not from Danny, especially not after the great day they'd had together. She was saying good-bye to so many important, wonderful things in her life right now, and a rejection from Danny would kill every other joyful memory she'd ever had of North Pole.

"Kiss him, Elda," someone else yelled.

Elda leaned toward Danny, and Holly ducked her head, shielding her eyes, allowing herself to disappear into the crowd as she made her way toward the door. This was perfect. Her two favorite people in North Pole were finally getting together. It was what she'd wanted all along. She repeated that over and over in her head, drowning out the voices of people cheering Danny and Elda on.

Chapter Sixteen

Stupid mistletoe. Stupid Christmas. Stupid North Pole.

Danny had spent most of this holiday season being annoyed by tourists and carolers and the froofy drinks he had to make at Santabucks, but he'd forgotten about the mistletoe, probably because, in the past, it had never been an issue. He'd always had someone to kiss. There was no question.

But tonight he'd found himself under the dreaded mistletoe, and his heart had pounded from nerves and excitement. He no longer had a girlfriend. He was a single guy standing under this blasted plant. And there was definitely someone he wanted to kiss.

And it wasn't the girl standing next to him.

His glance had snapped to Holly automatically, and Danny's thumb had gone to the tip of his forefinger, which had touched Holly's cheek before, a few days ago, during the second round of the gingerbread contest. He hadn't forgotten about it. When they'd made skin-to-skin contact, his nerves had lit up like the Griswalds' house. The two of them might cause a town-wide power outage if their lips touched.

But Danny had conveniently forgotten to consider the other person in this scenario. Elda was the one he was supposed to be with. She was the one her grandma had urged him toward and who had drawn pictures of him in her notebook. She'd remembered for eight years that his favorite candy bar was a Take 5. She liked him. Holly did not. Holly had cut him off when he was about to ask her out, and she'd made sure he and Elda sat together tonight.

And, you know what? Talking to Elda tonight was easier. It was better. He knew what to expect from Elda now, and he'd stopped waiting for the girl from their text messages to show up. He was starting to appreciate her for her.

He should kiss Elda.

Holly was the one who'd told him to stop thinking and just go for it. That was what he should do.

And then someone shouted, "Kiss him, Elda!"

This was the moment of truth. Danny gazed into Elda's big brown eyes and leaned toward her. He hadn't kissed anyone since Star. Heck, he hadn't kissed anyone before Star. This was a big moment. He prepared himself to remember it.

Elda, however, sideswiped his cheek and whispered, "You don't want to kiss me."

The crowd groaned with disappointment over the non-kiss for a split second before resuming whatever they were doing—drinking eggnog, returning skates, taking selfies with the life-size cardboard cutout of North Pole native and professional hockey player, Stan Stashiuk.

"Yes, I do." Danny was trying to grab the bull by the horns here. He and Elda were supposed to be together.

She caressed his cheek. Nothing. No sparks. Not a one. "No, you don't."

"I do, Elda. Our texts." They were going to make this work.

"Texting with you has been great," she said, "but...

Danny...our date wasn't."

"It was good. We had fun." Danny Garland didn't fail at stuff. He wasn't going to fail at this relationship before it ever had a chance to get off the ground.

"I think we might have more fun with other people," Elda said. She squeezed his shoulder, and that was it. Elda was done with him.

Danny nodded a tacit good-bye and hustled out of the building as fast as his crutches could carry him. He stood on the steps for a moment, squinting from the myriad of Christmas lights and the gold and silver aluminum ornaments decorating the trees outside the rink. Tourists and townies alike passed by—all paired up and gazing at their partners lovingly. Everyone around him was in a couple. Tonight was an exact replica of when he caught Star and Phil together in the laser tag room. Danny was the only loner in North Pole. He headed toward the comfort of Santabucks.

Danny had nearly started sobbing on Main Street when he caught Star kissing Phil. But the end of this whatever romance with Elda only numbed him. The fact that they couldn't make things work wasn't the worst part of the situation. Two girls had rejected him in one week. Oh-for-two, Danny was in a slump.

Elda squashing their budding romance proved he wasn't so special, that he was truly nothing without his ability to play basketball, that whatever "popularity" he'd built up over the past several years was all phony. Danny, outside his ability to shoot hoops, brought nothing to the table. Holly had known that about him right away.

Danny snuck a peek inside Santabucks before entering. He kind of wanted to talk to his mom right now. He needed to talk to the one woman on the planet who actually knew him. She was working the counter tonight, but she wasn't alone. Holly was in the coffee shop, too, and so was Craig.

They were sitting right next to each other, having a serious, intimate conversation. She leaned closer to Craig as he spoke. Danny's stomach churned. He was going to be sick.

They were on a date. At least it looked more like a date than whatever Danny and Elda had been doing on the architecture tour.

Danny, nearly choking on the oppressive scent of peppermint and roasted almonds that permeated Main Street, pulled his eyes away from the scene. He set off for home, keeping his head down to block out the Christmassy glow.

The breakup with Star had frightened him. When he met the Page girls, Danny should've done the irresponsible thing and thought with his heart instead of his head. He should've gone after Holly from the start. It definitely would've ended in disaster, but it would've been worth it. He should've thrown caution to the wind and beckoned her over to the mistletoe today, just to see what would've happened.

. . .

When Holly booked it out of the hockey rink to avoid having to watch Danny and Elda kiss under the mistletoe, she bumped into Craig in the parking lot.

"Where are you off to?" he asked.

Holly didn't have an answer. She was either going to hide or run or bury herself under a mound of royal icing and candy inside her grandmother's garage.

"I was gonna get coffee. Want to come?" Craig had his hands in the front pockets of his mom jeans, and he was rocking back and forth on his feet—heel to toe, heel to toe. He was nervous. Holly had never seen Craig nervous before. She figured him for someone who didn't care what other people thought.

Holly usually relished her solitude, but she needed a diversion. Craig had been fun at the arcade following the second round of the gingerbread contest, and she'd had a nice time chatting at the ice skating thing tonight. Grabbing coffee with him wouldn't be the worst thing in the world. It might actually be fun, keep her mind off other guys.

Plus, he had a car. An escape vehicle. She was on board with anything that would get her far away from the ice rink as fast as possible.

While Craig drove her to Santabucks, he kept talking about himself, the things he liked—movies and books and TV shows. Even though Holly couldn't bear to hear one more trivia tidbit about *Game of Thrones*, she didn't totally mind just listening. The distraction was working. Thanks to Craig, she'd forgotten all about Danny...for the moment.

As soon as Holly and Craig entered Santabucks, they were in Garland world. Danny's mom was working the counter. Danny's pictures were on the wall. This place unfailingly brought back memories of the first day Holly had seen him working here, The Coffee Shop Incident, of Holly adding Elda's phone number to his contacts, and of the two of them meeting here this morning before spending one fantastic day together. That was all in the past. Now he was kissing Elda.

She could totally picture it, the kiss. Danny and Elda were so awkward together, but all of that was just pent-up sexual tension. The mistletoe was the icebreaker. After that it was just a few quick steps to a full-blown romance.

Which was good, because that was the point of this whole thing. Elda needed someone worthy of her, and Danny needed someone who could open up to him and wouldn't break his heart.

Holly placed her order—medium cinnamon latte—and Craig jumped in to pay before she could.

"You don't have to," she said.

"I want to."

He was just being friendly. Craig had noticed that Holly was upset, and he was being nice. Holly accepted the drink, grateful for the kindness. North Pole was full of good people, people who looked out for one another. "Thank you."

"My pleasure."

After retrieving her drink from Danny's mom, Holly walked over to a table in the middle of the coffee shop, trying desperately to prevent her mind from conjuring up a mental image of whatever Elda and Danny might be doing right now. Holly was willing to bet they were at his house. Obviously his mom was working tonight, and they'd have the place to themselves. Holly shuddered as she reached for a chair. But Craig barreled over, nearly knocking her down, and pulled out a chair for her. Okay, so he was really leaning into this whole polite thing. "Thanks, Craig," Holly said as she sat down.

Then Craig took the seat right next to her instead of sitting across the table, which was super odd and intimate. Their arms were right next to each other, nearly touching. She kept her eyes down on her drink, because if she turned her head, she and Craig would be practically nose to nose. She wrote it off as Craig being incredibly socially awkward, which was something Holly could empathize with. It probably hadn't even occurred to him to take the seat across from her.

He kept talking about *Game of Thrones* for a few more minutes, and Holly worked hard to appear interested. When he stopped to breathe, she asked, "Is your showstopper ready?" Holly stared at the dried splash of coffee on the lid of her drink. It was shaped kind of like a reindeer, because of course it was.

"I'm about finished," Craig said. "It looks amazing. I'm really proud—" He cut himself off. "But how is your showstopper doing?"

Holly stared at him for a beat. "It's good."

Craig, blinking, tilted his head as if ready to hang on her every word.

"Craig? Is this a date?"

He straightened up. "Oh."

"I mean, if it is"—oh my God, what if it wasn't and she was saying all this right now?—"I want to be upfront with you right from the start. I'm not interested. I like someone else."

"Danny," Craig said right away.

"Yeah." Yikes. Maybe she'd been more obvious about her feelings than she thought.

"I always thought you two made more sense together than him and Esmerelda." Craig straightened up, resuming his usual air of disdain for other people. "Besides, it's fine. Dinesh thought you and I might make a good couple, but I get the feeling you don't really like *Game of Thrones*. I can't be with a girl like that."

"Good, well, we're on the same page." Holly sipped her drink, waiting for Craig to move to the other side of the table. He did not.

After she finished her coffee, Holly dragged herself home to work on her showstopper. At least the caffeine jolt would keep her up all night. She needed every available second before judging started tomorrow at four.

But she reached a roadblock just outside her grandma's house. A couple stood on the walkway, silhouetted in the moonlight. Holly's heart was in her throat. It was Elda and Danny. They were standing close, talking, touching each other here and there like they were constantly checking to make sure the other was real.

But wait. This guy wasn't wearing a cast, and he wasn't using crutches. It was Dinesh. Dinesh was touching Elda's hair and whispering in her ear. Elda was gazing at him like he was the Mona Lisa, and she was determined to figure out all of his secrets.

Holly marched right up to them. She pushed Elda's shoulder, not hard, but firm enough so Elda would know she meant business.

"Hey." Elda rubbed her arm. "What's the matter?"

"What's the *matter*?" Holly stared hard at Dinesh.

Elda ran her fingers through her hair and gave a slight smile to Dinesh. "Dinesh and I..." Elda grinned harder and shrugged.

Holly snapped Elda out of her Dinesh-induced haze. "Where's Danny? What about the mistletoe?" Holly shuddered. She'd been picturing Danny kissing Elda for the past half hour.

Elda squeezed Holly's hand. "I shot him down."

"You what?" Holly snatched her hand back. That wasn't how this was supposed to go. Elda and Danny were supposed to be on his couch right now rounding second base. It was the scenario she'd been preparing her brain for.

"Holly, I told you. Danny and I have nothing in common." She nodded toward Dinesh. "I found someone who doesn't mind the real me."

Dinesh leaned in. "I more than 'don't mind' her, to be clear."

Holly folded her arms. "But the mistletoe. I saw you move on Danny like you were going to eat his face off."

Elda laughed, her eyes wide with surprise. "I don't know what you thought you saw, but it wasn't that. I kissed him on the cheek, just to take the pressure off. He doesn't like me. If anything, I think he likes you."

"I wish you'd stop saying that." Holly's hands balled into fists, and she glanced over at Danny's house. The light was on in the front room, but she couldn't see in. "Danny Garland doesn't like me." Holly saw the truth when Danny had looked at her tonight. The word "nope" had been written all over his face.

"He's confused," Elda said. "Think about it. He's had this fabulous time texting with a girl he thought was me while having a great in-person rapport with you. His mind must be all jumbled up. We really did a number on him." Elda reached over and picked a bit of fuzz off Dinesh's coat. The two of them were chatty, bubbly, happy. They had an easy vibe that was the exact opposite of how Danny and Elda acted when they were together.

Dinesh wasn't the guy Holly would've picked for her cousin, but what did Holly know? She was the nerd who'd been in love with a guy for eight years, but instead of being honest and telling him about it, she'd tried to set her cousin up with him instead.

They really had done a number on him. Holly had concocted this elaborate scheme with literally no escape plan and no favorable ending. She had been messing with Danny this whole time, and it was time to make things right. Time to tell him the truth. Danny would probably hate Holly forever because of it, but it was the only possible way out.

"We've got to come clean. Both of us." Holly held out her hand. "Give me your phone. Please."

Elda handed it over.

Holly opened the text conversation with Danny. She wrote, "I want to explain everything. Meet me in my grandma's garage when you get this."

Chapter Seventeen

Danny glanced out the kitchen window toward the back of Mrs. Page's house. Holly and Elda were walking together to the garage.

Hadn't Elda already explained everything, or at least tried to? She wasn't into him. Period.

He shut his curtains and sat on his bed. What was left to discuss?

Almost immediately after he sat down, he stood again. He grabbed his crutches and went to the window. The light was on in Mrs. Page's garage. He touched the windowpane, which was cold under his fingertips.

He'd been all upset after his first date with Elda because he thought he was going to have to live his whole life pretending to be someone he wasn't in order to get girls to like him. But being around Holly today, he realized that wasn't the case. Some girls—or, at least one girl—totally got him. He was both totally comfortable and completely off-balance around her. He wanted to hold her and talk to her. He wanted to know her and wanted her to know him.

He knew she didn't feel the same way, and that she was possibly interested in *Craig*, but that was okay. He'd take the risk and tell her how he felt. She had to know. She was leaving in a week, and this couldn't go unsaid.

Elda had said in her text that she needed to explain everything. Well, so did Danny.

Danny's stomach filled with butterflies as he threw on a jacket, grabbed his crutches, and headed out the back door. He was super nervous, but he'd dealt with enough disappointment in the last month to know he could handle it if Holly ended up laughing in his face. He'd survived a broken leg and catching his girlfriend cheating on him in public. He could handle a little rejection.

A few months ago, he might not have been able to say that.

When he reached the garage, he peeked in the window. The door was slightly ajar, so he could hear the girls' conversation. Danny smiled to himself when Holly's voice reached his ears.

"Oh my God, you're hopeless!" Holly was laughing, tilting backward in a lawn chair, popping M&Ms in her mouth.

Elda was on the floor, fiddling with one of those gingerbread kits they'd used to practice for the second round. She was trying to make the walls stand, but they kept toppling over as she tried to add more icing.

Danny raised his hand to knock. He held his breath. This was it. This was the moment of truth.

"I mean, look at you." Holly laughed louder, covering her mouth to stifle it. "I can't believe Danny actually bought that you were the one who knew how to build a gingerbread house."

"Shhh," Elda said. "Shut up."

And now his breath was stuck in his throat. His hand had stopped about an inch from the door. For once, Danny was glad to be on the crutches, because at least they were keeping him upright.

"Besides, I'm not that bad." Elda leaned back, admiring her handiwork.

"You're terrible," Holly said. "You suck."

"Well, *you're* a terrible matchmaker." Elda's voice lowered to a whisper. "Texting him all that stuff about architecture and weird books? No wonder we never had anything to say to each other."

Danny's heart skipped a beat, and the past week or so started replaying in his mind, but with a new clarity. Holly rocking the second round of the competition, telling him she was a sculptor, an artist. Elda having absolutely nothing to say to him whenever they were together, but Holly being able to see into his soul.

The girls had been playing a prank on him. He'd been talking to Holly this whole time.

And he was a dumbass not to have seen it.

They were literally laughing at him right now.

He rapped on the door. It was an involuntary action. He wasn't sure if he was making his presence known or trying to get them to stop saying these things.

Both girls' heads swung toward the door. The dim lighting in the garage cast dark shadows on their faces. Danny pushed the door open the rest of the way and stepped inside.

Holly jumped up from her chair. "Danny." He got the sense she was about to rush toward him but caught herself when she saw the look on his face. "Oh."

He swallowed, trying to quell the emotion rising in his throat. "So, I heard what you were talking about just now." He gripped the handles on his crutches so hard, his fingernails dug into his palms. "You two were messing with me this entire time?"

"No." Now Holly moved toward him. Danny tried to step

backward and almost fell. She stopped in her tracks. "We were not messing with you."

"Honestly," Elda said.

"Oh? *Honestly?*" They were acting like all of this was totally normal, like playing a guy for a fool was no big deal, like Danny should be totally cool with this very normal news.

"We never meant to hurt you," Holly said. Her eyes were black in the dark garage. She'd folded her hands in front of her chest like some fourth grader who'd gotten caught cheating, like she was begging for forgiveness.

"You never *meant* to hurt me? Well, everything's fine then. All is forgiven." Danny wasn't normally so sarcastic, but the tone seemed to fit the situation. He'd come here armed for rejection, but he should've come prepared for humiliation instead.

"I'm so sorry," Holly said. She was near tears. Good.

"I can't believe you did this, knowing everything that's happened to me over the past month. All the time you were pulling this crap—pretending to be your cousin on the phone, trying to get me to like Elda, because…?"

"Because I like you, Danny." Now Holly was crying. Her lip trembled, and her breath was shaky.

"No, you don't. You don't knowingly deceive someone you care about." A few hours ago, hearing Holly say those words would've sent him to the moon, but now he only felt like a rube.

Holly closed her eyes, and the tears kept rolling down her cheeks. Elda ran over and wrapped an arm around her cousin. "This is so hard for me to say," Holly said.

"Maybe text it to me."

Holly opened her eyes. They were still in shadow, but their emotion cut through the darkness. "I only did this because I was too scared to tell you how I felt. Someone like you was never going to want someone like me."

"What does that even mean, 'someone like you?'" He wanted to fold his arms in defiance, but he had to settle for gripping his crutches harder.

"You're popular and outgoing, completely out of my league."

"Well, that's ridiculous," Danny said. Since the day they met, Danny had been thinking Holly was out of his league.

"Also"—Elda let go of Holly and stepped forward—"I told Holly I liked you, and she was just trying to help me not say things about dead squirrels."

Holly gestured to her cousin. "You and Elda made more sense. Believe me, I've been rejected enough times to know that. I knew I couldn't stand it if you looked at me like other guys do. It'd crush me. I've liked you since we were eight."

So much wasted time. If she'd just told him at the holiday gala or put her own damn number in his phone, all of this could've been avoided. He would've leaped at the chance to be with Holly. But instead of being honest about her feelings, she'd tried to pawn him off on her cousin.

"You know what, Holly? Maybe the reason people reject you is because you pull garbage like this instead of being honest." His brain was a jumble of confusion. Part of him was ready to forgive Holly on the spot, but a bigger piece was hell bent on making her feel as shitty as he felt right now.

"Danny," Elda said, "that's a low blow."

"No, Elda," Holly said, "he's right. I know it'll never be enough, but I'm so sorry. I got in too deep. I was just going to help Elda strike up a rapport with you, but I took it too far. It was like, I'd always wanted to talk to you, and I got carried away when I had the chance. I didn't want to stop. I mean, we'd chat for hours."

He raised a hand to stop her. He couldn't hear any more, not right now. Those chats had been the best thing that had happened to him in the past month. He lived for feeling his phone buzz in his pocket, knowing it could be her on the other end. "But it was all a lie. Everything between us was one big lie." He turned toward the door. "Good luck with your showstopper tomorrow. You're gonna need it."

. . .

Holly ran up to the attic after Danny left, and Elda followed her. Their entire family was watching a movie in the living room, and all of them turned to watch Holly storm up the stairs.

"Are you okay?" Elda asked after Holly had flopped facedown on the pull out couch the two of them had been sharing. Elda sat gingerly next to Holly's legs.

Holly, still on her stomach, turned her head toward the wall. She let her eyes unfocus, and the plaid pattern on the pillow in front of her took on a 3-D quality. She'd just been rejected by Danny Garland, but not in the way she'd anticipated.

"I blew it," Holly said. "I completely blew it."

Elda patted Holly's leg. "He'll come around."

"No, he won't. And even if he does, I don't know how to do this. I don't know how to be honest with someone about how I feel. I've been pushing people away for so long that I don't know how to let anyone in. Texting with Danny while pretending to be you was the most open I'd ever been with anyone, and it was utter bullshit."

"Imagine if you'd been honest with him right from the start."

Holly sat up. She was face to face with her beautiful, perfect cousin, who had no idea about anything. "Let me tell you what would've happened, Elda: He would've said thanks, but no thanks. He would've told me he didn't see me that way, and that we should just be friends. I've heard it a bazillion times. I let my guard down, and here I am again, crying into a pillow. I'm done. I'm out."

"Is this how you're going to live the rest of your life?" Elda asked.

Holly nodded.

"You're going to keep every single guy you meet at arm's length because you're afraid of getting hurt?"

Holly nodded again. "That's the plan."

Elda lightly punched her cousin's knee. "No offense, but that's absurd."

Holly shrugged.

"I mean it. It's ridiculous. You're telling me you're simply going to sit there and accept loneliness for the rest of your life?"

"It's better than being hurt over and over again."

"Life is pain, Holly."

Pain. What did Elda even know about pain? Holly pointed to the stairs. "Says the girl who could walk out on the street right now and get a million guys' numbers without even lifting a finger."

"You know what?" Elda stood. She waved her hands in front of her chest. "I'm done with this. Danny didn't turn his back on you because of some imagined knock against your looks. He walked out because you've been misrepresenting yourself to him this entire time."

Elda was right, but ugh.

"And," Elda said, "you're beautiful and unique. You've got an edge that I'll never be able to pull off. Here's your real problem: no one in his right mind would ever want to be with someone so closed off and defeatist."

Oh, freaking please, Elda. "Can I have a second to wallow, please? I just had my heart broken."

Elda folded her arms. "One second. Literally. No more."

Holly drew in a deep breath and immediately blew it out.

"Okay, you good?"

Holly nodded.

"Super," Elda said, "because here's what you don't seem to understand. You are an awesome person. Yeah, maybe I'm blond and skinny, but honestly, I'd give anything to have your brains or your funky style. Plus, you were always Grandma's favorite." Elda's eyes brimmed with tears, and she tightened her arms around her chest.

"Elda, don't cry." Holly wrapped her arms around Elda.

"I've always been the pretty one, but you were always the cool one."

"Oh, fuck you." Holly laughed, nudging her cousin away.

Elda laughed, too. "I mean it. You were, like, too cool, above it all. You've never cared what other people think."

"Not true," Holly said. "I think I care too much sometimes, and that's part of the reason I tap out socially the way I do, because if I put myself out there, it will show people exactly how cool I really am not."

"Well, cool or not, you were the one with the big ideas and the imagination. You were the one who'd get the good grades and who Grandma would brag about to her friends."

Holly scrunched up her nose. "No, she didn't." This was news to Holly.

"Oh, she for sure did. I've heard it a million times since we've been here—'Oh, are you the one Dolores used to talk about all the time? The one who liked architecture and gingerbread houses? No? Well, never mind then.' They have no time for me."

Holly put a finger to her lip, tracing the line of her scar, which was weirdly numb, like the nerves had never properly healed. It matched the lack of feeling in the rest of her body. She was in shock—cold, dead shock. Not only had Holly driven Danny away, but apparently her grandmother had been bragging about her to her friends. Guilt was the only sensation leaping from nerve ending to nerve ending. She should've come here more. She should've made the time.

Life was too, too short.

Elda patted Holly's knee. "Grandma had apparently been trying to set you up with Danny Garland for years, not me. You. Because she knew you and Danny were right for each other."

Holly started to say something, but Elda cut her off. "Also, I'm used to guys looking at me all the time. I know the 'he wants me' look you're talking about. Danny never, ever gave me that look, but he was constantly checking you out."

If Elda was right, then Holly had definitely become so guarded and insecure that she was totally missing the signs guys were allegedly sending her.

Holly sighed. Her breath was shaky. "Well, I screwed up, didn't I?"

"Maybe not." Elda stood up again, arms akimbo, like the superhero she was trying to be. "You spent the past week texting him for me; I'm gonna go talk to him for you."

Holly jumped up and blocked the stairway. "No, no, no. I don't need you to fight my battles. It's what got us into this mess in the first place, right?" She had to do this on her own, for real. It was the only way she could ever possibly make things right with Danny. "Give me your phone." She held out her hand.

"Again?" Elda cautiously placed her phone in Holly's palm.

Holly pressed the four-digit code on Elda's phone. "I'm just going to get his number out of your contacts. I'm going to text him, but this time I'm doing it as me."

Chapter Eighteen

HOLLY: *Hey, Danny. It's Holly. Call me when you get a chance. Please.*

HOLLY: *I am so incredibly sorry. You have no idea. Actually you probably do.*

HOLLY: *The truth is, I'm bad at opening up to people. I suck at putting myself out there.*

HOLLY: *I've been looking at my grandma's day planner tonight, and it's like...she lived her life. She took risks. Maybe I need to take more risks.*

HOLLY: *(Game of Thrones "Come at me, Crow" Night King gif)*

HOLLY: *I should know better than to try to curry favor with you by sending you GoT gifs. I'm sorry for that, too. I realize by now that you're not going to call, so I'll just take the risk and say this: texting with you, spending hours every night getting to know the brain of THE Danny Garland? Best time of my young life so far.*

Chapter Nineteen

Sunday, December 24

Danny had been right. Everyone played games, and everyone had an angle. He was never going to find someone with whom he could just exist, be himself, let his guard down. He'd thought he'd found that person in Holly, but nope. She'd been playing him the whole time.

Holly kept texting him all night from what was allegedly her own number, but Danny ignored the texts. After the first one, he didn't even bother reading them. He'd turned off his phone so he didn't have to hear another word from the Page girls.

The next morning, he dragged himself to his team's basketball game out at the Countryside tournament. Or, really, he didn't drag himself. Brian dragged him. Given a choice, Danny would've stayed far away from that place. The North Pole High basketball team was so far from his reality right now, and, frankly, he wanted nothing to do with it. He didn't want to see Phil Waterston in his seat on the bench, or

Kevin taking Danny's spot on the floor, or Star cheering the team on from the sidelines. It was all part of a world Danny no longer belonged to.

But he kind of did want to get out of North Pole for a while, so he went, leaving his phone at home.

Brian dropped him off at Santabucks after the game, around one. Danny had promised his mom he'd work the afternoon shift until the third round of the gingerbread contest started at four. Brian had offered to bring Danny's showstopper over to the town hall, so all Danny had to do was show up on time...where he would come face to face with the Page girls, whom he'd been avoiding all day.

He was on edge during his whole shift. Every time the bell above the door rang, Danny startled, worried that it'd be either Holly or Elda or both. He'd have to face them sooner or later, and he was banking on later. After today, he planned on hiding for the next week, until they left town. He'd stay in his house and play video games or something. It'd be fine.

But then the Santabucks bell rang, and in walked Elda with Dinesh. It wasn't fine. She was glaring right at Danny. Dinesh had to stop her from lunging at him.

"So, you're here," Elda said. "You're alive."

Danny walked over to the register and leaned on his crutches. Elda was a customer, nothing more. And that's how he'd treat her. He didn't owe her anything. Not one stinking thing. "What can I get you?"

"Nothing," she said. "Did your phone die or something? Did you drop it in the toilet?"

"We have a special today on eggnog lattes," he said.

"I'll try one of those," Dinesh said.

Danny grabbed a cup and went over to the espresso machine.

Elda muttered to Dinesh, "We're not ordering anything."

"But I want one. He owes me. I let him into laser tag with

his broken leg."

"I'm on it, Dinesh." Danny started making the latte. At least it was something to keep him busy, something to focus on instead of Elda's angry eyes.

"Holly stayed up texting you all night." Elda stood behind the espresso machine, peering around it to see Danny better. He still refused to look up. "She was trying to apologize, trying to tell you her side of the story."

"You want whipped on this, Dinesh?" Danny knew Holly's side of the story. She and her cousin had spent the past week or so pranking Danny, not even caring what it did to him.

"I know you think you're the victim here, but you're no less to blame than Holly."

Danny glared at her as he placed Dinesh's drink on the counter. How dare she? How dare she stand there with her hands on her hips like Danny wasn't the one who'd had his heart trampled on. "Oh, really?"

Elda rested her hands on the counter. She and Danny were almost nose to nose. Her dagger-like fingernails were pointing right at him. "Yeah. Really."

"How am I even remotely to blame for this situation?"

"Because you were never genuinely interested in me. You wanted her the whole time."

Danny staggered backward a bit. He blamed his crutches. "You have a lot of nerve, Elda." He focused on putting a lid on Dinesh's cup.

"I could tell you were vibing on her right from the start. I only went along with Holly's plan because you were cute, I needed to shake up my romantic life, and Holly insisted she wasn't into you. I bought her lie because she's an evil genius, but I saw right through you. You were looking at her dog tattoo the day we spoke at the dance."

He narrowed his eyes at her. "Yeah. I noticed a tattoo.

As people do."

"Oh, but it was more than that. You never had two words to say to me. You were always checking her out when we were together. She's the one who made you laugh."

Danny shrugged. None of that meant anything, because it didn't erase the fact that they had sold him a bill of goods posing as his dream girl.

"Instead of being honest with her—or me, for that matter—that Holly was the one you wanted, you kept up this charade that you had a thing for me when you most certainly did not."

Well, she had him there.

"Frankly, I should be the one who's pissed off. You could've broken my heart," Elda said. "Or I could've kept pursuing this thing with you and missed out on meeting Dinesh." She wrapped an arm around Dinesh's shoulders.

She had a point, but she was leaving out a key piece of information. "Elda. You never liked me, either."

"True." She rested her head against Dinesh's shoulder.

"So, we're all to blame. We all screwed this up," Danny said.

"Not me. I'm blameless." Dinesh pointed to the pastry display. "So, I'll take a cinnamon crunch muffin with my latte."

Danny reached for the tongs.

"Yup. We're all to blame," Elda agreed. "But blame is a waste of time, my friend. Holly and I are only going to be here for one more week, then we're gone. You could stand here blaming her, or you could go to her, forgive her, and spend the next week making out with a girl you're totally attracted to."

Between "make out with Holly" or "not make out with Holly," the former definitely sounded a lot more fun. "I've already tried the whole dating a girl who treats me like garbage thing. Not recommended." He handed Dinesh his muffin in a bag.

Elda reached across the counter and squeezed Danny's hand. "Yeah, Holly was texting you under someone else's name, but that was the only thing fake about it. She showed you who she was. She opened up to you more in the past week than she's ever opened up to anyone."

Danny glanced out the window. People were filing past, heading to the town hall for the gingerbread contest. He checked the Rudolph clock on the wall. They still had a little time, today and until Holly left North Pole for good. Frankly, they'd wasted enough time. "Where is she?"

"Home." Elda raised her eyebrows. "She felt so bad about hurting you that she's forfeiting the gingerbread contest."

His heart sped up. "What? No. She worked so hard—for herself and your grandma. She can't just give up."

"That's what I told her, but she wouldn't listen to me."

Danny glanced at the clock. It was three-thirty. The competition was due to start in a half hour. His mom should be here at any minute to take over his shift, but Danny had to do something. Now. He couldn't just let Holly give up. "Okay. Anybody have a car? Dinesh?"

He shook his head. "Sorry, man."

"Shit." He scanned the people passing by on the street. Danny was looking for something, divine intervention. They didn't have time to walk to her grandma's house and get back to the town hall. "You can run, right?" he asked Elda.

"Better than you right now, probably."

"Touché." He reached for his jacket under the counter. "Here's what we're gonna do. You run to the town hall. Tell my brother Brian to take his car, pick up Holly's showstopper from her garage, and bring it to the competition as fast as he can. Then you stick around and stall the mayor for as long as possible—make something up."

Elda clapped. "Now this is a plan I can get behind."

"Dinesh," Danny said, "I need you to stay here and watch the shop until my mom gets here in a few minutes." He zipped up his hoodie. His body wanted to bolt, to run as fast as humanly possible over to Holly's grandma's house. A clock ticked in his head. They'd already wasted too much time, and he had a set of crutches slowing him down.

"What are you going to do?" Dinesh asked as Elda bolted for the door.

Danny pulled the hood over his head. "I'm going to get Holly, obviously." As soon as he said it, he felt his lips pull into a grin.

Dinesh shot him a thumbs-up, and Danny scurried out the door. He was finally going to "meet" his dream girl.

• • •

Holly turned off the TV as soon as her family left the house. She couldn't find the remote, and she was not going to sit here in solitude and listen to Fox News talk about the war on Christmas. She flicked one of the metallic red balls on the tiny Christmas tree the family had set up on the coffee table in the living room. Christmas seemed to be doing just fine.

She grabbed Grandma's day planner and hauled it into the den off the kitchen. She took Grandma's spot at the desk and opened the cover. Holly hadn't spent as much time looking at this as she'd planned. She and Elda had done most of the things Grandma had scheduled for December, but it had become less about honoring her memory and more about just having fun in North Pole with Danny.

Holly glanced over at Danny's house. It was dark. She checked the cuckoo clock on the wall. Three-fifty. The gingerbread contest would start in ten minutes.

She couldn't blame Danny for not texting her back last night. She was an utter failure when it came to romance.

Maybe someday she'd find someone who'd be able to deal with it, but today was not that day.

After flipping through the music on her phone, Holly slipped on her headphones and turned the volume all the way up, losing herself in Taylor Swift's own personal melodramas. TS was Holly's go-to broken heart playlist. She thumbed through the pages in Grandma's calendar. It was a symbol of the impermanence of life. Holly was only eighteen years old, and already she was being forced to say good-bye to her grandmother, this house, this town, and a perfect dream life she'd created in her mind.

She'd cried about her grandmother after she died, of course; but in public, she'd always tell the story with a smile and detached pride about how Grandma died. "She was lying by the pool in California with a Moscow Mule in her hand. So badass."

It was badass. And it was awesome that her grandma didn't suffer, that she'd lived a long life, that she'd stayed healthy and was able to enjoy life until her last day. But it so, so fucking sucked that Holly didn't get to say good-bye. And it so, so, so fucking sucked that Holly was such a failure as a granddaughter, especially now that she knew her grandmother had been bragging about her to her friends and trying to set her up with the incredibly cute boy next door. Holly could've made the time to visit North Pole. She could've asked her grandma more questions about her life and her past. But she hadn't. Not because she didn't care, but because she'd gotten so used to cutting herself off from people. It had become such a habit that she even managed to cut off her grandma, one of her favorite people on the planet.

Grandma should've died knowing for sure how much Holly cared about her. Holly should've told her. Now it was too late.

And here she was, repeating the same mistakes, just on

a smaller scale.

She wasn't silly enough to think that she and Danny Garland were meant-to-be or some nonsense, but, still, his existence had profoundly affected her life. He was the one, indirectly, who got her thinking about studying architecture as a career. Now that they were older, he was one of the few people on the planet who understood her, and who wanted to understand her. She'd screwed that up, as well.

And now she was sitting here alone, blowing out her eardrums, avoiding Danny again. The final round of the competition was starting. A tear rolled down her cheek. He deserved to win again, and he deserved happiness. It was what she'd been trying to bring him all along.

Resolved, she stood and pushed her grandma's chair back in. She turned up the volume on one of Taylor Swift's more powerful anthems, letting the music fill her. She'd go watch Danny win. She'd cheer him on and expect nothing in return, but she'd show him definitively how much he meant to her, how much she truly hoped he was happy. She couldn't leave North Pole without him knowing.

With the music still pumping, Holly pulled on a pair of shoes and a jacket and opened the front door. Danny Garland, mid-knock, nearly fell right into her arms.

And Holly nearly fell into his. Her knees faltered, but she managed to step backward. She ripped off her headphones, and a ringing filled her ears. She could hear the blood pulsing through her body.

"I've been knocking forever," he said.

Oh my God, was he cute. The two of them might never be this close again. He was leaning forward, his hands gripping the handles of his crutches, and he had a slightly crooked smile on his lips. His sky-blue eyes, however, betrayed his nervousness. Holly was pretty sure hers did, too.

"I was listening to music." She said that too loudly. Her

ears were still recovering from Taylor Swift's voice blasting against her brain.

Danny was still smiling at her. He shouldn't be smiling at her.

She dragged her eyes away from his lips and focused on her grandma's old mailbox off in the distance. "Danny, I'm sorry."

"I know."

"But I want to say it." She still couldn't look at him. This was uncharted territory for Holly Page.

She took a deep breath. That was the old Holly. The new Holly told people how she felt no matter how scary it was. "You mean a lot to me, Danny. I know that's weird, but I got into architecture because of you, because you made me up my game in the gingerbread contests. I studied math and angles and structure. I read books about architects and architecture. As a kid, I'd always loved drawing and sculpting and stuff, but it was because of you that I found the art in buildings." Now she looked at him. Some unrecognizable emotion settled in his eyes. Old Holly would've written it off as confusion or revulsion, but new Holly saw it as something different—he was concentrating, listening. To her. "I just wanted to thank you for that."

He let that hang there for an agonizing beat, then he said, "I used to sit by my front window during Christmas break waiting for you to show up. I'd tell people I quit doing the gingerbread contest because I was too busy." He rolled his eyes. "But it was really because you weren't there. Why bother competing if my biggest rival wasn't going to show up?"

"I used to dream about coming back here. I had, like, intense daydreams that I'd show up in North Pole and you'd remember me and, well...happily ever after." Holly sighed. "The first day Elda and I ran into you at Santabucks, it crushed me. We had this bizarre encounter; you had a girlfriend. But the worst part was, you didn't even remember me."

Danny grinned. "I didn't recognize you. But I did notice you."

"You did?" Holly's heart sped up.

"Oh my God, yeah." His broad shoulders shook as he laughed. "Don't you remember how awkward I was?"

"But you kept looking at Elda."

"She had chocolate on her face. And she was talking about roadkill."

Holly laughed. Elda would be mortified.

"And I kept looking at her, Holly, because I was trying not to look at you. I had a girlfriend at the time."

"Right."

He leaned closer on his crutches, and Holly shuffled forward slightly, closing the gap between them. "When I saw you at the dance the next night, I couldn't stop thinking about how hot you were with your tattoo and your cute little scar. I wanted you, Holly, but you wanted nothing to do with me. I just got out of a relationship with another girl who didn't like me. I didn't want to make the same mistake again."

"It was self-preservation," Holly said. "I was scared you'd reject me."

"I wouldn't have rejected you."

He was so close now, leaning toward her, studying her face. She hadn't been this close to a guy in, well, ever. She could physically feel that he wanted to kiss her. The tension in the air pulled the two of them together. Holly's first instinct was to laugh and run. She didn't know how to do this. How did kissing happen?

"I'm under the mistletoe." His eyes went to the ceiling above him.

Holly looked up, too, and she laughed. It was this old sphere of wax mistletoe that her grandmother had always kept strung up on the porch "just to make things interesting."

Grandma had been gone a month, and she was still pushing Holly and Danny together.

He smiled at her again, and Holly wasn't sure what she was supposed to do. Her normal response would be to laugh it off, like "ha-ha, mistletoe is a joke," a defensive reaction to avoid the embarrassment of the guy not wanting to kiss her. But Danny Garland had brought it up. He was standing under the mistletoe looking at her like she was Elda or somebody. Or, no. She had to stop thinking like that. Danny had never looked at Elda like this. He liked Holly. He wanted Holly.

She could get defensive, run and hide, or do something about it.

She stepped closer to him. "Is there any safe space in this town?" She tried not to think about her lips, or licking them, but they were absolutely the only thing on her mind.

"Perils of living in a Christmas village. Mistletoe grows wild here," he said.

"How unfortunate." They were so close now that Holly's chest was about a millimeter from his. Holly's blood pumped hard through her body, sending terror and excitement to every one of her fingers and toes. She was about to kiss Danny Garland. She willed her brain to stop thinking for just the tiniest moment. She leaned in and pressed her mouth against his.

His lips turned her insides to liquid. She relaxed, trying to simultaneously turn off her brain and capture every single moment for posterity. Whatever happened next, she'd go home to Chicago and make many, many collages, sketches, and sculptures about this moment. Danny Garland kissing her.

Danny whispered in her ear, the tip of his perfect nose tickling her skin. "Even better than I imagined."

"Same," Holly whispered. She hugged him close, resting her head on the outside of his arm, gazing out at the view from her grandma's porch, the mailbox, the familiar cars lining the street. The neighbors across the road had put out a gigantic Wonder Woman blow-up lawn ornament. She blinked a few times to make sure she was actually seeing what she thought she saw. Yes. Little white flakes danced in the light of the street lamps, which had just clicked on.

She lifted her head from Danny's shoulder. "Wow, Danny. We made it snow."

Chapter Twenty

It was snowing, and Danny was kissing Holly.

He didn't believe in Christmas miracles, but kissing this girl under the mistletoe on Christmas Eve during the first snowfall of the year felt pretty close to one.

Kissing Holly was a whole new thing. Danny had only ever kissed Star, and that had become routine. They knew each other's moves, every step in the repertoire. When he and Star got together it was like a choreographed dance. They were a Vegas act that had been performing together so long, they could do the show practically half-asleep.

He had to stay alert with Holly. She felt different in his arms. She was softer and shorter than Star. He felt powerful holding her and leaning down to touch her lips. His skin kept lighting up in different spots—this was new, this was exciting. This was euphoric.

He leaned back and held Holly at arm's length. "We have to get to the town hall."

"Right." She grinned. "You're about to be champion again."

"I don't know. Craig's gigantic *Game of Thrones* wall is pretty impressive."

Since it was snowing and they were already very, very late, Holly helped Danny load his crutches into the back of her family's minivan. After she stuck the key in the ignition, she turned to him. "We kissed." A smile was glued to her face. She tried to do that thing where her tongue played with her top lip, but her perma-grin prevented it.

How could he have ever believed this girl didn't like him, that she'd treat him like garbage? And why had he let himself believe that? She was only here for another week. He could've let her go forever without telling her how he felt. He could've gone his entire life without knowing what it was like to hold Holly Page in his arms. That was a terrifying thought. "Want to do it again?"

She leaned closer to him, and their lips touched. They only gave in for a second, breathing each other's air. "We really need to go." Her mouth was still touching his when she said it. "I don't want you to miss the blue-ribbon ceremony."

"Right." Now he was wearing a perma-grin. She had no idea he'd had Brian pick up her showstopper. Holly could really win this thing. As much as Danny loved trophies, he wanted that for her. And for her grandmother.

"So," she said as she pulled away from the curb, "is it too soon to ask what now? I mean, we kissed. I'm leaving. What the hell are we doing?"

He held out his hand, and she laced her fingers in his. Their hands belonged like this. They fit together perfectly. "Let's take it slow, all right? Let's not talk about what we are or aren't. I'm holding Holly Page's hand, and that's enough right now."

Holly grabbed one of the employee parking spots right behind Santabucks, and they dashed down the street—as fast as Danny's crutches could carry him. Holly threw open the door of the town hall, and the two of them hurried inside, where they were greeted by applause and cheering. Danny startled, glancing around, trying to figure out what was going on. Had he won the contest? Had Holly?

But no. The crowd wasn't cheering for them. Everyone was looking at a big screen in the back of the room, upon which was playing a slideshow of Holly's grandmother. Elda motioned for the two of them to sit next to her, and they did.

As the slides flew by behind him, the mayor stood up on the dais and said, "We lost one of our own this year, one of our most enthusiastic gingerbread competitors, Mrs. Dolores Page."

Everyone clapped.

"Dolores embodied the spirit of North Pole. She was a great neighbor and a great citizen. She participated in every event—even the Stash Grab contest last year, where she won third place. Dolores loved her friends and her family. We're so glad to have some of them here tonight."

Danny checked on Holly and Elda sitting next to him. The girls were holding hands, and a tear ran down Holly's cheek. Danny, feeling inadequate for not having a tissue or a handkerchief, handed Holly the scarf from around his neck. She smiled and dabbed at her face.

"People come and go from this town all the time, and there are only a few constants, the real townies. This year we lost one of those pillars of our community, and she will be missed."

The mayor turned around and watched as the slideshow continued to play.

"This is the memorial Grandma would've wanted," Holly whispered.

"She totally would've dug it," Elda said. "She loved this place more than anything."

Danny turned to them. "Your grandma." He shook

his head. "I can't even imagine someone else living in that house."

"Us either." Holly's other hand grabbed Danny's.

He'd experienced so many recent life changes that losing his elderly next-door neighbor had seemed like one of the smaller ones. But Dolores had always been there for him, Brian, and their mom. She had their spare key. She invited them for dinner once a month, at least. He mowed her lawn and weeded her garden in the summertime, and she made him cookies and lemonade as a thank you. And now someone else would've been living in her house. Dolores was gone. Her family was leaving and never coming back.

But he couldn't get all sad about it now. Holly was here for another week. They still had a bunch of holiday festivities to get through. Now was not the time to be sad. Now was the time to be grateful for all the things he did have, the things he could've very easily missed out on if he hadn't allowed himself to open up. He squeezed Holly's hand, and she squeezed back.

The mayor stepped up to the microphone again. "It is time now to announce the winner of this year's gingerbread contest."

"Wait. Is that my showstopper?" Holly pointed to the table at the front of the room, where all the competitors' entries had been displayed.

"I may have had my brother sneak it out of your garage," Danny said.

Holly squeezed his hand and didn't let go.

"In third place." The mayor squinted at the card in front of him, then looked up, grinning. "Tinka Foster!"

Tinka stayed in her seat for a moment, frowning. But then she leaned over and hugged Sam before trudging up to receive her award.

"In second place...my goodness, our own Craig Cooper."

Craig's jaw dropped. So did Danny's. If Craig was in second place, that meant...what? That Brian hadn't gotten Holly's entry here on time? That'd she'd been disqualified for bringing in a late entry? He glanced over at the display table. His basketball court was great but couldn't hold a candle to Holly's house. She should not lose on a technicality. Danny was about to run up to the podium in protest, when the mayor started speaking again.

"And in first place, winner of the coveted gingerbread trophy, the Stanley Cup of North Pole, plus a one-hundred-dollar gift certificate to Joyeaux Noel is..."

Holly squeezed Danny's hand tighter. "Get ready."

Danny would decline the trophy. He'd say, "Thanks, but no thanks," and hand the prize off to Holly. She deserved it. Danny hated losing—absolutely hated it—but even more than that, he hated winning an unfair fight.

The mayor opened the envelope, looked at the card, whipped off his glasses, and wiped them. Then he read the card again. "Well," he said, after a moment, "this is unprecedented. We have a tie. The Page girls and Danny Garland!"

Danny dropped Holly's hand in shock. "We won," he said. "We both won." Holly handed him his crutches. Oh, yeah. He still had to go up and receive his prize.

Holly tried to pull Elda up, but she wouldn't budge. Grinning, she folded her arms and remained in her seat. "You go up alone. The prize is yours, not mine."

"It's our family's."

Elda shook her head. "You take this one. You earned it."

Holly helped Danny stand, and the two of them ascended the dais to receive their awards. Danny marveled at the one-eighty his life had taken in the past twenty-four hours. He'd gone from thinking Elda was his soul mate to accepting his life as a loner to kissing Holly. And now the two of them had won the gingerbread contest. As they stood together, taking pictures for the newspaper, Danny leaned down and whispered, "There's only one trophy, you know."

"I know." Holly smiled as a flash nearly blinded them. "Who gets it? I mean, me, obviously. You've had it before. This is my one chance."

"But you have to return it before the next competition. It's a traveling trophy. You don't get to keep it. And you're never coming back to North Pole." He tried hard not to think about that, but it was the truth.

"Maybe I'll have to make an exception." She nudged him in the side. "You know, to preserve the sanctity of the gingerbread competition."

As they finished their photo op, Dinesh rushed the stage and grabbed the microphone. "Everyone," he said, "I have something I need to do." The entire crowd gawked at him. Dinesh wasn't known for his loud proclamations. He usually let Craig do the public speaking, if not the karaoke. "I..." He trailed off as if seeing the crowd for the first time and remembering that microphones terrified him.

Craig ran up and put an arm around his buddy's shoulders. "What he wants to say is, Esmerelda—"

Dinesh snatched the mic back. "I have to do this myself. Elda, I know we just met, but please stay here in North Pole. With me. I—" Dinesh got down on one knee.

Holly gasped. "Holy shit."

"Indeed," Danny said. Today would be etched in the North Pole history books—the first tie in gingerbread contest history, and now the first proposal.

"Will you marry me?" Dinesh asked.

The crowd cheered as Elda jumped up and ran to the dais. "Yes, yes, *yes!*" she squealed, pulling her new fiancé into a massive, smothering hug.

"When Elda makes up her mind, she really makes up her

mind," Holly said, clapping for her cousin and Dinesh.

Danny leaned down and whispered, "Looks like you'll have a reason to come back here again."

Holly clutched the trophy hard to her chest. "Which means I am definitely taking this home with me."

Chapter Twenty-One

Tuesday, December 26

HOLLY: *I'm on my way. I swear.*

DANNY: *The movie's about to start.*

HOLLY: *I KNOW. The grownups are making Moscow Mules in honor of Grandma, and my uncle made Elda and me run to the store for limes.*

HOLLY: *(gif of kids from Love, Actually saying "I hate Uncle Jamie")*

DANNY: *It's fine. I'm keeping your seat warm…for now.*

HOLLY: *Oh, no! If I don't make it in time, who will you give my seat to?*

DANNY: *Well, Craig's been eyeing it.*

HOLLY: *Damn it, Craig!*

HOLLY: *I'll be there in five. Ward him off.*

. . .

12:15 AM, New Year's Day

DANNY: *When can I see you again?*

HOLLY: *I literally just left your house. I'm not even back at my grandma's yet. I'm texting you from your front porch.*

DANNY: *But you're leaving in the morning.*

HOLLY: *Not until lunchtime.*

DANNY: *Have breakfast with me...before we part FOREVER. (sobbing emoji)*

HOLLY: *Not forever. I'm coming back for Elda's wedding.*

DANNY: *Feels like forever.*

HOLLY: *You know, my phone works in Chicago, too. We have cellular towers and everything. It's a pretty big city.*

DANNY: *You mean we can keep doing this whole texting thing?*

HOLLY: *I mean...yeah. I'd like that. No pressure, though.*

DANNY: *No pressure. But, like, if Craig did something silly that I just HAD to tell you about...*

HOLLY: *You could text me.*

DANNY: *Or if, say, I had a question about what to watch next on Netflix?*

HOLLY: *Text.*

DANNY: *I suddenly feel so much better about this whole "you leaving" thing.*

HOLLY: *I'm going to bed. See you tomorrow morning!*

DANNY: *Happy New Year! [heart eyes emoji] Good night!*

HOLLY: *Good night!*

. . .

Ten minutes later

DANNY: *Okay, what should I watch on Netflix?*

HOLLY: *All right. Let's figure this out…*

Chapter Twenty-Two

Thursday, January 18

"You know I wouldn't do this for just anyone," Holly said, gazing deep into Danny's beautiful blue eyes. She'd made sure to touch up her makeup and fix her hair after school. It had been snowing today in Chicago, and her cheeks were still pink and cold from the wind.

"I know. You told me before you'd never, ever FaceTime for me. I thank you for loosening your rules just this once."

"Well, it is a special occasion." Holly propped her phone up on the desk, perched on her chair, back straight, and waited.

Via the magic of FaceTime, all the way from his house in North Pole, Danny lifted his leg and plopped it onto his kitchen table.

"Danny, we eat there," came his mom's voice from off screen.

"I know, but just for a second." He peered into the camera at Holly. "Check it out. No cast."

She clapped as he removed his pale, skinny leg from the kitchen table. "How does it feel?"

"Light," he said. "And weak. I have to do physical therapy now, to strengthen it, but it's coming along. I'll be ready to walk the streets of Chicago soon enough."

He was coming down to Chicago for spring break, which had been planned pre-Holly. He wanted to check out Loyola, one of his top college choices, and maybe a few other schools, too. Holly wondered how much she'd get to see him when he was in town. She didn't want to assume. But the way he talked about the trip, it sure seemed like he planned on hanging out.

Danny was staring at something off screen now, and Holly tried to guess what it was. Soon, however, Danny's eyes were back on her. He leaned in close to the screen, unselfconscious, because he was Danny Garland and of course FaceTime-ing was no big deal for him. He probably hadn't fretted at all about how his hair looked or whether or not the angle of the phone made his face look fat. Holly had tried desperately not to worry about that stuff herself. Danny liked her as she was. Old habits died hard, though, hence the makeup. Plus, this was their first time seeing each other "in person" since Holly left North Pole on New Year's Day.

"Hey," he whispered, "you look beautiful, by the way."

"Why are you whispering?" she whispered back.

"My mom's just over by the counter."

"And she can still hear every word out of your mouth," came his mom's voice.

Holly grinned. He called her "beautiful" in front of his mom. Sure, it was kind of embarrassing, but it was also kind of awesome. "How are Elda and Dinesh doing?"

Danny nodded toward the kitchen window. Elda and Dinesh, thanks to Dinesh's sizable down payment from all the money he'd saved working at the arcade and living with his parents, had bought Grandma's house. They'd moved in a few days ago. Elda had spent the weeks leading up to the move updating the plumbing. "They're good. They've been sending Craig over to me whenever they want some alone time."

"Sorry."

"It's not so bad. We play video games, and we've started watching *Game of Thrones*."

"Nooo! Traitor!" Holly squealed in mock horror.

"You'd actually like it," Danny said.

"I probably would, but don't tell Craig that."

Danny mimed zipping his lips. "I wouldn't want him to suddenly decide he's in love with you because now you know who Beric Dondarrion is."

Holly's face flushed. He'd said "love." "Who?"

"Let's keep it that way."

"What else is new?" Holly leaned back in her chair a bit. This FaceTime thing didn't suck. It was kind of like she and Danny were chatting in the same room. And Holly had almost forgotten to worry about how she looked on screen. Almost.

"Well, the basketball team is still in first place in our division, and Coach is finally letting me help out. I joined the engineering club at school, if you can believe it—"

"I can."

"—but they're hazing me right now, since I'm the newbie. How about you?"

"I'm going to look at a few colleges in Indiana this weekend with my parents. Nothing too exciting. My friend Rebel and I are working on a new art show, too." Holly had created several pieces for this one. And she planned to display them more prominently, instead of shunting them off to a dark corner somewhere. "You want to see what I'm doing?"

"Of course."

Holly held up a mosaic of Christian Laettner she'd crafted

out of tiny pictures of his, and Duke's, biggest foes. It was quite an undertaking and had required a lot of research on her part. Thank goodness she now knew a Christian Laettner expert.

"I want it," Danny said, making grabby hands.

"One million dollars." Holly clutched it to her chest. She'd had an art awakening ever since she got home. She'd been seeing her surroundings with fresh eyes—picking up all kinds of debris and shiny objects on the sidewalk. Yeah, she was still going to study architectural engineering in school, but she'd keep going with the art thing, too. No reason she couldn't do both.

"Hey," Danny said. "I miss you."

"I miss you, too." They'd had a great week after Christmas. A perfect week. They'd made all kinds of plans to do the traditional North Pole stuff during the remainder of her visit, but opted instead to spend time together hanging out, only bothering to do stuff when they absolutely felt like it. They hadn't made any promises to each other, and when she left on New Year's Day, she questioned where they stood. It would've put too much pressure on their little baby relationship to make any big proclamations. They weren't Elda and Dinesh, after all. They were still in high school, and they were making plans for college, plans that didn't involve the other person.

But then they'd started texting, and Danny called her, and then she called him, and suddenly it became a thing they did, not out of obligation, but because they wanted to.

And, boy, did she look forward to those phone calls.

"I can't wait to meet Rebel," Danny said. "You know, when I'm in town."

"Oh, yeah. You want to meet her?" A smile teased Holly's lips.

"Sure. I mean, as long as you're there, too."

Holly shrugged. "I guess I can come."

"If you have time, of course," Danny said.

"Of course."

Danny checked his watch, and the air went out of Holly's lungs. *He must be looking for an excuse to get off the phone.* That was the problem with video chatting, seeing all the stuff people tried to hide when they were just talking on the phone. But then he said, "Three…two…one."

Holly's doorbell rang.

"You should probably get that," he said. "And take me with you."

A lump in her throat, Holly took the stairs two at a time down to her front door, which she flung open. Rebel stood there with a massive bouquet of pink roses.

"These are from your…Danny," she said. "I don't know."

Rebel handed the flowers to Holly and stepped into the house.

Holly, without worrying about how she looked, held the phone up to her face. "Oh my God."

"I've been doing some thinking," Danny said. "This long-distance thing stinks, but it's what we've got going right now."

"It does stink," Holly said, relieved that he was the one who brought this up.

"We're seeing each other in March for spring break, and in June for Elda's wedding, but I think we need one more visit in between, at least." He smiled, but his eyes were unsure, nervous. She made Danny Garland nervous.

"Like, so, would you be interested in coming up to North Pole in May?"

"In May?"

"For prom." He winced, waiting for her answer.

Holly hugged the flowers to her chest. "I'd love to."

Danny still smiled, but relief also painted his face. "It's a date, then."

When she and Danny got off the phone, Holly went right to her day planner. She'd bought it when she got home from North Pole, and it was just like the one her grandma had used. Holly loved the fact that it was paper, tangible. She could run her fingers over the words.

She skipped ahead to May and recorded the date of Danny's prom. She'd ask him to hers, too, of course, and maybe to come down to Chicago sometime this summer. And when they were both in college—him here, maybe, her in Indiana, probably—they'd make plans to meet up whenever they could, for as long as they wanted.

Life had no guarantees. Holly knew that. She'd seen that firsthand when she found her grandma's journal. But the days, weeks, and months went by no matter what anyone did in the present. The future was a mystery, a big beautiful mystery. Hope lived inside these blank pages, and magic, and potential beyond Holly's wildest dreams, as long as she stayed open to the possibilities.

Chapter Twenty-Three

March

DANNY: *I'm stopping at Culver's for lunch. Should I get a Butterburger or a grilled chicken sandwich?*

HOLLY: *If you even have to ask…*

DANNY: *Joking. [Sends picture of a double Butterburger with cheese]*

HOLLY: *Phew. We can still be friends.*

DANNY: *Friends? Aren't we beyond that?*

HOLLY: *[Insert blushing emoji]*

DANNY: *I can't wait to see you!*

• • •

HOLLY: *Are you lost? I hope you're not lost.*

HOLLY: *You know my house is off of NORTH Harlem, not South, right? You put the right address in Google Maps?*

DANNY: *I'm driving! Are you trying to kill me with all these texts?*

HOLLY: *No. Stay alive, please.*

HOLLY: *You should've been here forever ago. Ugh. I'm sure traffic on the Kennedy is garbage. It always is. I'm not worried. Not worried at all.*

HOLLY: *Remember you can hop off the Kennedy and take the Edens if that looks better.*

DANNY: *You Chicagoans and your dumb expressway names.*

HOLLY: *Not dumb, awesome. Just, you know, send me an SOS text if you're in trouble.*

DANNY: *Hey, Holly! Call off the search party. I'm here! :)*

Airing of Grievances

As this is a holiday book, I'd like to honor Festivus and take a moment to not thank the following people/entities:

Any airline that refuses to hand over a full can of pop on a flight from Chicago to Seattle. Oh, really? This half a cup of liquid is supposed to sustain me for the next four hours? Thanks, buddy.

The Sims and *SimCity* for being too much of a distraction. I HAVE THINGS TO DO.

George R. R. Martin.

Avocados for being so delicious and so expensive.

Cheetos for being so delicious and so bad for me. (See also: cake, pie, Pringles, Take 5 bars, 100 Grand bars, cheese popcorn, etc.)

My favorite nail clippers. Where have you gone?

The Bulls for letting Jimmy Butler go.

Mosquitoes.

About the Author

Julie Hammerle is the author of *The Sound of Us* (Entangled TEEN, 2016) and the North Pole, Minnesota YA romance series (Entangled Crush, 2017). She writes about TV and pop culture for the ChicagoNow blog, Hammervision, and lives in Chicago with her family. She enjoys reading, cooking, and watching all the television.

Discover more of Entangled Teen Crush's books...

JUST ONE OF THE BOYS
a novel by Leah and Kate Rooper

Alice Bell has one goal: to play for the elite junior hockey team the Chicago Falcons. But when she's passed over at tryouts for being a girl, she'll do *anything* to make her dream a reality... even disguising herself as her twin brother. With her amazing skills on the ice, Alice is sure she'll fit in easily. That is, until she starts falling for one of her teammates...

THE UNCROSSING
a novel by Melissa Eastlake

Luke can uncross almost any curse—they unravel themselves for him like no one else. Working for the Kovrovs, one of the families controlling magic in New York, is exciting and dangerous, especially when he encounters a curse involving Jeremy, the sheltered prince of the Kovrov family—the one boy he absolutely shouldn't be falling for. Jeremy's been in love with cocky, talented Luke for years. But Jeremy's family keeps deadly secrets, dividing him between love and loyalty as a magical war starts crackling. This might be one curse Luke can't uncross. If true love's kiss fails, what's left?

BREAKING THE RULES OF REVENGE
an *Endless Summer* novel by Samantha Bohrman

Mallory is tired of being the girl who stays home and practices French horn while her identical twin, Blake, is crowned homecoming queen. So when she has the opportunity to pretend to *be* Blake, she takes it. At camp, she'll spread her wings and emerge a butterfly. Or at least someone who gets kissed by a cute guy. That is, until bad boy Ben shows up, ready to get revenge on Blake—aka Mallory.